SWING AWAY

A LITTLE LEAGUE NOVEL

CHRISSY WISSLER

BLUE CEDAR PUBLISHING

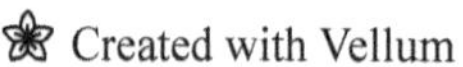 Created with Vellum

Hidden in Fire

Hidden in Flight

Hidden in Spirit

Hidden in Desire

Hidden in Memory

Hidden in Time: Novel

Hidden in Lore: Collection #1

Hidden in Myth: Collection #2

Hidden in Legend: Collection #3

Enchantment Avenue

Searching for Sanctuary: Novel

Dragons in Preschool: Short Novel

The Blessings Bridge

Pixie Dust Cupcakes

Christmas Weather Witch

Unfreeze a Heart

More than Nurture

Romance Video Game Series

Second Chance: Novel

Anything Possible

Changing Perspective

ACKNOWLEDGMENTS

I'd like to thank both of my parents, for believing in me, for never laughing at my hidden dreams of being a writer, and also for putting so much time and money into my softball career. I may not have wanted those big dreams, but I found something just as worthwhile—writing. Thank you for showing me how to fight for my dreams, especially when someone else told me I wasn't good enough. Thanks also goes to my at home companions—to Ally, who needed her walk every day and got me out of the house, to Timothy for making me laugh like only a parrot can. To Sean, my rock and my support. And most importantly, thank you to my readers. To each of you who enjoyed my short story, "Prom Dates & Softball Bats," which this novel was based on. And thanks to those of you who stumbled upon this story for the first time.

ONE

Jenny didn't bother hanging her mom's handmade curtains, the same curtains her mom made *every* time they moved. After all, what was the point?

She glanced at the bright floral designs, like someone had exploded a garden onto the fabric, cringed and tossed them back into the moving box labeled 'Jenny's Stuff.'

She scowled at the other half-dozen boxes, hands on her low-riding jeans as her iPod cycled through to the next song. Hell, what was the point of even unpacking?

"Because there is no point."

Not when her dad could wind up with another stupid team at the end of the season and then poof! She'd be in a new city, a new school… and on another damn softball team.

From her cracked open door, she heard her mom humming in the kitchen two stories below, followed by the familiar crashing and tinging of copper pots being hung, of silverware finding a new home.

Home.

The silverware probably had a better idea of what 'home' meant than Jenny did. At least the plastic tray they stayed in remained the same.

Unlike Jenny and her whole damn life.

The phone rang and her mom's voice changed from normal to excited.

Dad was calling.

Jenny kicked the nearest box with a booted foot. Well, *she* wasn't excited. Not about him calling and not about them moving.

Again.

"And they can't make me unpack."

So, she didn't. She threw her long brown hair into a ponytail, slapped on a baseball cap (this one from the team her dad ditched two months ago), turned the music up, and shoved first one box, then another into a corner.

By the time her mom hung up (not like Jenny was actually listening —even though she had one ear bud out), Jenny had finished 'unpacking.' She surveyed her room, worrying her bottom lip, and tried not to think about how dull it looked.

But dull was okay, right?

After all, no sense getting cozy if she'd be up and moving in another handful of months.

"Jenny! Your dad called." Her mom poked her head in, her smile dazzling and bright. A smile Jenny only saw when Dad decided to grace them with his presence. "His plane just landed from Arizona. No more spring training and no more putting off family time."

Her smile fell when she noticed the boxes neatly stacked between Jenny's bed (yes, she at least had made it—even tucked in the damn sheets) and her bare closet.

And no, she hadn't actually bothered to hang anything.

Let her shirts get wrinkled for all she cared. It wasn't like she was trying to make an impression, or hell, even make *friends*.

"Jenny."

Her mom opened the door the rest of the way, then mirrored Jenny as she stood with her hands on her hips. "I thought I asked you to unpack?"

"I did."

There was a slight pause, a pause only accented by her mom's diamond earrings as they glinted from the southern California sun as it struck unhindered through the un-curtained windows.

Curtains her mom noticed piled on top of the boxes. "I know this is hard on you."

"No, you don't."

"It's hard on all of us."

"No, it's not."

Because Dad liked to come home bearing please-forgive-me gifts, like the diamonds her mom now wore.

Okay, maybe that *wasn't* quite fair. Never in her life would Jenny want to be in her mom's shoes, but still… her mom was also an adult. An adult, by the way, who was fully capable of putting her foot down and saying enough of this bullshit.

She didn't, of course. And Jenny was fairly certain the diamonds had something to do with it.

Jenny, however, had absolutely no control over her life. No control of where they moved, of which school she transferred to, or hell, even which softball team she played for.

Why? Because she was sixteen freakin' years old, and right now, even her ability to drive was vetoed at the whim of her dad.

But if there was one thing her mom insisted on, it was control over the household life.

Like curtains.

Her mom's lips pinched into a tight line, but she said nothing about the curtains and instead hung them up herself. The sun's glare was suddenly cut off and Jenny couldn't help but see how her life felt the same way.

"I know this is hard," her mother said again, "but I know this time it'll be different. You should have heard your father on the phone. He's excited. He can't wait for Opening Day, can't wait to take us both down to the clubhouse."

"Uh-huh. Right. You mean, he's more excited than he was for Chicago? Or Pittsburgh? Oh, and how about San Diego?"

San Diego had been their most recent 'home' -and their most recent move. And with dear Dad in spring training for six freakin' weeks, it once again left Jenny and her mom to do all the damn packing.

She *hated* moving.

"Jenny." Her mother jerked the curtains in place, like she was going for the perfect curtain arrangement or something. Whatever. "You're not making this easy."

"Gee, I sure wouldn't want to inconvenience you or something."

"He's got a real opportunity here. The Anaheim Chargers really wanted him," her mother continued, "and this is a real shot for your dad to make it big."

From where Jenny stood, staring out a three-story mansion overlooking the beautiful coast, she didn't think you could get much bigger in Major League Baseball.

Other than bigger checks.

Which, to put it bluntly, was Dad's reason for accepting the deal with the Chargers. Sam Taylor, the newest hot thing in baseball (and highly sought after), had taken to being a free agent like a dog takes to peeing on every single freakin' bush. And let's face it, he'd wrung out the Chargers for every cent he could.

And even though it was a three-year, couple-million dollar deal, Jenny knew in this game three years didn't *actually* mean anything. What it meant was they *might* stay in one location for three years. But the odds of that actually happening?

Let's just say getting traded to some other team half-way across the country was more likely.

Her mother finally finished with the curtain, and stood in front of Jenny. She tugged the remaining iPod ear bud from Jenny's ear and her familiar, comforting music vanished.

Her mom even placed a hand on Jenny's shoulder as if her touch would make it better.

Well, it didn't.

Life didn't work that way anymore. In fact, it'd stopped working like that some time ago. Like when she was five.

No more kissing bruised knees would make *her* life better.

"Aren't you at least going to try? Don't you want to fit in?"

"What's the point?" Jenny stepped back and her mom's hand fell. "How many friends have I left behind? How many schools have I been to in the last two years?"

Jenny felt traitorous tears swelling in her eyes. She absolutely refused to cry about this!

Her mom sighed. "I'm disappointed in you. This can be an opportunity for you too, if you let it. But if you don't readjust your attitude you'll never be happy."

"Happy? Like you?" Jenny slammed her mouth shut but the words were out.

They hung in the air between them, cold and hurting. Her mother looked away first. She reached up, lightly touched one of her diamond earrings. As much as Jenny was mad at her mom for putting up with Dad and his bullshit, she also didn't want to hurt her.

There were certain 'things' Jenny didn't mention to her mom.

And there were certain 'things' her mom very carefully ignored.

Her mother straightened, smoothing out her dress and trying to smile, trying to act like what Jenny had said was no big deal at all.

They both knew better.

"Mom —"

"It's fine, Jenny. I know this is hard on you. It's hard on all of us."

"Except Dad."

Her mother said nothing.

Like it or not, they were a family, and at the end of the day the only person Jenny had—who Jenny *could* rely on—was her mom.

She couldn't rely on her dad. And lately, she couldn't even rely on softball. Even the small spark of joy she used to feel the moment she stepped onto the pitcher's mound, breathed in all the sights and sounds of the game, of when she pitched the first ball of the game… even that had disappeared.

Faded.

And she didn't know why.

From the corner of her eye, Jenny noticed the shining, gold-colored tip of a trophy sticking up from one of the boxes. Her most recent trophy, the one her team had won at the Tri-Ace 16 and Under Tournament in San Diego. One of many, many trophies and the only stupid reason it wasn't packed away with the others (and the legions of dust they'd gathered over the years) was because of Dad.

Dad, who hadn't yet seen it yet. And then *after* he'd smiled, preened and pleased with himself and his legacy daughter, it'd get shoved away with the others. After all, her trophy collection didn't warrant the kind of attention *his* did.

Jenny tossed her iPod onto the bed and reached to slam the cardboard flap back down to cover the trophy. She didn't make it. Not before her mom saw it.

"Oh! Your trophy."

It was like seeing Jenny's trophy had flipped a switch. Like it gave her mother permission to smile again, to wave away the tension in the air like it was a cloud of too-expensive, stale-smelling perfume.

Her mother rescued the trophy from the stack of boxes and actually wiped off the 'Congratulations Winner' engraving with the hem of her dress. "You should bring this down. Your father can't wait to see it."

She didn't *want* to show him the damn trophy. "Why? It's not like it matters."

"Of course, it matters. Jenny? What's gotten into you?"

Now, Jenny could list several pages of 'what's wrong' and 'what's gotten into her'—starting, of course, with the move. Then she'd throw in her mom's whole denial crap just for giggles. But she didn't because if her mom hadn't figured it out yet, a list sure as hell wasn't going to help.

"Nothing."

"Come on, let's go downstairs and wait. Your dad said he'll be here shortly." And like that, her mom forgot everything—their argument, that Jenny needed her 'attitude readjusted,' Jenny's snide comments about her dad and being happy.

As they waited in the 'foyer' (as her mom loving called what really was just a fancy living room), her mom prattled on about the Chargers and how she *knew* this time it'd stick for their family. And not only that, she was positive Jenny would make plenty of friends, would love living in Sunny View, and would never want to move.

"The only one who's going to be making friends is Dad," Jenny mumbled. Friends with different shades of *lipstick*.

"Did you say something, dear?"

"No."

Jenny tried not to vomit as her mom looked out the curtained windows from the living room for the tenth time (yes, even these curtains were handmade). But regardless of how long they waited, with her stupid trophy looming down at Jenny from the fireplace mantle, Dad remained a no-show.

At least until 4:00 in the morning.

TWO

Jenny felt a slight dip in her bed and she groaned, fighting her way out of another nightmare involving her standing on the pitcher's mound wearing nothing but Chargers underwear and a softball hat.

"Hey, kiddo."

The sound of her father pulled Jenny from her nightmare, which she was more than happy to forget. She rolled over, uncovering the pillow from her head with one hand and wiped at her crusted eyes with the other.

"Dad?"

"Who else?"

Her dad knelt beside her bed and a sliver of moonlight peeked through her curtained windows. She could barely make out his face. The same face that was currently gracing all the local magazines and newspapers, as if everyone needed to get the inside scoop on the newest baseball celebrity to move to Sunny View.

He was eye-level with her, unusual because he usually towered over her at his six-foot height. But now, down at her level, he seemed less grand, less… well less famous and more like her dad.

"What time is it?"

"Early."

Jenny glanced at her clock. Then she sat up as if she'd stuck her finger in an electric socket. "Four? And you're just getting home?"

"Sssh. Quiet. We don't want to wake your mom, do we?"

Jenny didn't care about waking her mom. In fact, her mom *should* be awake to yell at him.

She narrowed her eyes. "Where were you? You were supposed to be having dinner. With us. You know, the family you haven't seen in six weeks."

"A business meeting came up. I got the call on the road. I'm sorry. I should have called."

Business meeting?

Spring training was intense, games and practices every day—but they didn't go to 4:00 in the morning. Managers were crazy with the schedules, but they weren't stupid. Not to mention she had a pretty damn good bullshit meter and right now it was blaring in the very hot, very much red zone.

"Do you know how long we waited? Do you know how long Mom cooked that dinner?"

A four-course freakin' meal most of which was dumped into the trash. At least Jenny had saved the cheesecake. Not an easy feat considering her mom was on a rampage—chucking both the food and the dishes they were in. It was one of the rare moments of Carol Taylor's temper.

At least the meal was good. From what Jenny managed to shove onto her plate before Mom went crazy.

"I know. I know. I promise I'll make it up to you." He smiled at her, the special smile that was either 1. Used for interviews and reporters or 2. Used to appease Mom when she was spitting mad.

He knew better than to use it on Jenny.

"Gee. I'm not quite sure how you'll give us both three hours of our lives back, not to mentioned Mom's dashed dreams of this being a whole new, great life for us. But you're sorry so I guess that just makes everything better. Goodnight, Dad."

She thumped back down and turned her back on him.

"I've missed you. Not a day has gone by without me thinking about you."

She didn't budge.

"Come on, Jenny. Don't be like this."

"Watch me."

He, of course, didn't leave. He wouldn't until he'd said what he'd come here to say. After all, Sam Taylor didn't waste his time.

The bed dipped again as he shifted position. "I wanted to say hi."

"Fine. Hi. Goodnight."

"I saw your trophy."

Jenny clutched the blanket.

"I'm sorry I couldn't be there. You know I wanted to be, but with training… well, Chuck said you played great. And I know you'll play great on the next team he's got picked out for you."

She squeezed her eyes closed and tried hard not think about why her chest hurt, why she suddenly wanted to cry.

"He also said your Taylor Bat is coming along nicely. That you'll be smacking home runs into the outfield like your old man."

"I don't smack home runs." She wasn't a power-hitter like her father and never would be. Not like he ever listened.

"You'll see," he chuckled. "Just like you've got the Taylor Arm."

Right. She also had the Taylor Smile, the Taylor Wave and look pretty to the crowd, along with the Taylor Stubbornness.

That one she was at least proud of.

"Hard to know," Jenny snapped, "when you're never actually around."

"I'll be there this season. For you. You'll see."

"I'll believe it when I see it."

He never had time for her. He was always busy. And regardless of what he said, of how much he wanted to see her play, he never did.

And you know what? She was tired of trying to get his attention, trying to prove herself and how she really did have the Taylor Arm. She didn't want to be Sam Taylor's legacy.

She just wanted to be Jenny.

Ha. Like that was going to happen. Like he was going to *let* that happen.

"I promise, Jen. This week might be a bit hectic for me, with the season starting, but I promise I'll be there." He sighed when she didn't say anything, and then leaned over and kissed the back of her head. "It's good to see you, sweetheart. I've got something special planned for you. You'll love it. We'll talk in the morning, okay?"

She didn't want anything special.

She just wanted her dad.

The kind of dad who used to play catch with her. The kind of dad who taught her how to not throw like a girl. The kind of dad who loved his wife and daughter more than he loved baseball, more than the fame and money.

A real dad.

She didn't say anything and apparently he was smart enough to figure out she wasn't going to. He left, closing the door as silently as he came in. Jenny turned and watched a light flick on. She could hear the distant hum of voices.

So. Her mom had been up.

They wouldn't fight.

They never did.

Even now, Jenny could imagine the hurt look on her mom's face, the tears she held in by sheer force of will. Her dad would say nothing, would just kiss her cheek and tell her he missed her.

It wasn't until Jenny drifted to sleep, when her mind finally quieted, that she thought about her father's face in the moonlight… and the scarlet smear of lipstick on his collar.

"Welcome home, Dad."

THREE

J enny stared at her bowl of Lucky Charms cereal and yawned. The milk had turned a puke-brown color from how long the marshmallows had been sitting in it, but the last thing she wanted to do was eat.

Especially eating food that reminded her of happier times. Times when her dad was actually around. Times when *he'd* been the one to fill her bowl of Lucky Charms because he was actually there.

Her mom sat across from Jenny, Mickey Mouse coffee mug held close to her chest. "You're not eating."

"I'm not hungry."

"You look tired. Did you sleep okay? I know it's hard sleeping in a new place —"

"Dad woke me up."

"Oh."

Jenny waited a beat, waited to see if her mom would say something, if she would mention her own dark circles she'd tried to hide with make-up.

When the silence stretched between them, broken only by the drip from the coffee pot, Jenny pushed up from the table. "Forget it. I'm getting dressed. Chuck still coming?"

Her mom nodded. "I'll let him know you'll be outside."

"Whatever."

She stomped up to her room and glanced at her parents' closed bedroom door, where she could hear the deep growl of her dad's snoring. It must be a rare day off, otherwise he'd have been long gone before she got up.

An image of the night before filled her head, her dad leaning over her, kissing her goodnight… and then the brief glimpse of lipstick.

She slammed her bedroom door closed and threw on mesh shorts, softball socks, and grabbed her cleats, which she put on outside. Her mom hated getting clumps of dirt on the floor—whether the house's floor was carpet, fake wood, hardwood, or marble.

Jenny thumped down on the back porch and heard the rumbling of Chuck's truck pull into the driveway. Chuck always arrived on time, was always well-dressed and polite, and he never, ever showed up with lipstick on his collar.

He was also crazy fast.

By the time she finished tying her shoes and pulled her hair into a ponytail, Chuck was waiting in the backyard. He stood there in his loose, red, flannel shirt and a Chargers baseball cap on his head, a few strands of silver-gray hair poking out. He had a ball bucket overturned beside a net to catch her sometimes wild pitches, and a home plate placed right in front of it.

Not far off was the pitching mound her dad had ordered built for Jenny, complete with large square box filled with sand. Just like all the others in every house they lived in.

If, of course, you counted a couple months as 'living' there.

She didn't.

"Mornin,' Jen. Rough night?" Chuck grinned at her, warm and friendly, but today she couldn't feel any warmth—as if it was being sucked out of her soul or something.

It probably was.

"Yeah. Something like that." Jenny shoved her glove on. "The usual?"

Chuck's grin faded. He nodded. "Nothing fancy today. Let's just get you warmed up."

"Fine."

She didn't care. Not really.

Why should she when every day of her life was the same? Chuck showed up. She practiced. She pitched. She hit. She fielded ground balls. She hit the dirt. She pretty much did every lesson her dad could imagine for her own personal softball trainer.

That's right. A softball trainer. One her dad paid well enough to move right along with them.

But Chuck wasn't her dad, the one who *should* have been passing on all those 'Taylor Legacy' secrets he liked to tell the press. Then again, she was so mad at him right now that if he was sitting there she'd throw a screwball right at his nuts.

Jenny rubbed her right shoulder, the muscles already tightening. This was also becoming routine. Whether she thought about her dad or thought about softball, her muscles got tight.

She breathed in, dug her cleats into the dirt and pitched a curve ball. A curve ball that absolutely didn't curve. Again. For the sixth one in a row.

Chuck made a face—meaning the slightest thinning of his lips— and tossed the ball back. She barely caught it before she was turning on her cleats and stomping back to the mound.

The last thing she wanted to do was practice softball—softball, which the older she got, seemed to matter less and less.

Like her and unpacking… what was the point?

She practiced, she played, and what did it matter?

Even if she killed herself to be the best softball player ever, practicing every free minute she had, it wouldn't change anything. Her dad would still be too busy for her. He still wouldn't care enough to show up to her games.

Finally, after another five minutes of horrible pitching, Chuck tossed the ball into his glove. "I think that's enough for today. You wanna tell me what's on your mind?"

"There's nothing to tell. The usual."

Chuck frowned, then grabbed his bucket and tossed both his glove and the softball in. "Already at it, huh?"

"Yeah. Already."

Chuck nodded. He wasn't an idiot and could put two and two together. Like Jenny not sleeping well and her dad still in bed.

That, and Chuck had been around the family enough to know what went on inside the mansion's walls.

Jenny snorted. As if you needed insider knowledge. All anyone had to do was read the damn tabloids and they'd know everything that went on in her dad's life.

She glanced at the house, saw her mom's bobbing form in the kitchen window. She also a heard a door softly close and knew her dad had finally gotten up.

Jenny tightened her grip on her glove, remembering his talk from last night, remembering the lipstick and more of his empty promises. She didn't want to talk with him.

She lingered by Chuck, neither of them walking towards the house. They just stood there. Waiting.

She also remembered her dad mentioning the team Chuck had picked out for her. Jenny briefly closed her eyes. So it would start. All over again.

"You gonna tell me about the team you picked out for me or should I do a Google search on Sunny View."

Chuck's eyebrows lifted. "I'm surprised you haven't done that already."

She shrugged. "It didn't seem important."

And it wasn't. Important would imply that she had some say in the matter.

"It's important, Jen. Otherwise why are we here, doing this every day?"

Now it was her turn to lift her eyebrows. "Because my dad makes us."

Chuck smiled. It was a toothy grin. Not a happy one. "We can still both say no."

He could. She couldn't.

And she didn't want to think about that right now. She leaned down, untying one of her cleats. "So you going to tell me about them?"

"The Sunny View Tigers. They've got a good team, but haven't hit the championships yet. A bunch of their star seniors are graduating this year and one's nursing tendonitis in her arm. I thought it'd be a good place —"

"For me to make my mark. Shine."

"There's nothing wrong with shining."

No. But there was something wrong with purposefully searching for teams that made Jenny look even better, made her irresistible to the scouts. The way to attract attention was being on the winning team. If you stood out on a winning team, well, more than a few calls would come your way.

At least she thought so.

"You're a good ballplayer," Chuck said, "and they need someone with your talent. It's a good match. And from the way this season's starting off, they could use you—your pitching and your bat."

"Right. A good match. Like stacking my softball resume had nothing to do with it."

"If you want, we can go watch them play. Give you a chance to get a feel for them."

"Yeah. Like what I 'feel' matters." Jenny stomped towards the back door, froze, then stomped back. "Hold on. You mean today? Today's Sunday. High school teams aren't allowed to play on Sunday."

Chuck's shoulders shook as he let out his deep chuckle.

"You know something." She poked a finger at his chest. "You know this team."

"It just so happens I might. They might also be a well-known travel team who *is* allowed to practice on Sunday."

"A travel team?" The best of the best, playing out of state, out of country, and she'd been on her fair share. "A travel team who also happens to have the same high school players?"

"Possibly."

It was a chance for Jenny to glimpse her new life… even if it wouldn't matter in the end. Still, it was more chance than she ever had before. A chance to maybe, in some small way, have control over one piece of her life.

Chuck slipped his hat off and scratched his head. "You can see them play or we can call it a day. It's your call, Jen. Your choice."

Her choice.

Jenny's stomach twirled with something that felt suspiciously like hope, and, maybe, an ounce of freedom.

FOUR

When Chuck pulled up to the Sunny View Sports Park with its four softball fields, Jenny knew what to expect. Tough team, dedicated, cutthroat players who wanted a shot at the biggest scholarships to the most prestigious college schools.

That was the world of softball.

Jenny's world.

She didn't need a scholarship (her dad had the cash to pay for tuition), but money wasn't the point. The point was the prestige, the team placement, and it was her dad who wanted it. He wanted it badly enough to put Jenny on all the best and up and coming softball teams; the kind of teams who shared the mentality of 'there's no 'I' in 'TEAM'—but there is a 'ME.'

But when Jenny glimpsed the *Angels* team through the truck window this wasn't what she expected. Practice didn't start until 10:00, but at 9:30 there were a good handful of girls pulling on cleats and stretching in the outfield. Not to mention, it was Sunday morning and there were quite a few people headed for the softball fields.

"Is this practice or a game?"

"Practice." Chuck switched off the engine. "Why?"

"They can't all be parents." She nodded to a couple dozen people.

"Fans. Mostly."

"Fans? Fans don't exist in high school and they most certainly don't exist for *travel* teams."

"You sure 'bout that?"

Chuck got out and waited for her by the curb. He had that look again, the excitement of being at a softball park. She couldn't even remember the last time she'd been excited about playing, about stepping onto the mound and throwing a game's first pitch.

"Okay," Jenny said. "Who are these guys and how the hell do they have fans coming to see them *practice* on a Sunday morning?"

"The *Slugging Angels.*"

He said it in a way that it explained everything. It didn't.

Jenny cocked her hip and placed a hand on top, which made her jeans sink a little lower. "I've never heard of them."

"Can't say I'm surprised, but this is what your dad pays me for. Come on. I think you'll be impressed."

They headed towards the field, Chuck moving slightly faster. Jenny had a hard time not dragging her feet. After all, this was just another team.

"Let's put it this way," Chuck said. "The *Angels* used to be a '12 and Under' team only because Coach Laurie didn't want the girls growing up too quickly. She'd been through the softball grinder, like you're going through, and pulled out when the pressure got too much."

"And… she came back as a coach?"

"Eventually. She started the *Angels* as a team who played for fun first, competition second."

"Makes sense why they stayed '12 and Under' then."

And it did. The second girls hit that special age of 14, the competition sky-rocketed. That fun game you used to play? You know, the one where you pulled your dad out of bed on a Saturday morning because you couldn't wait to get to the field?

Yeah, it was long gone by the time high school came around.

Chuck gave Jenny's ponytail a small tug. "Got that right. As soon as the girls got too old for the *Angels* they were off to another team.

Some took their coach's teachings to heart. Others, well you've met quite a few girls like that."

Cutthroats.

"Yeah, I know *all* about that."

"To make a long story short, and removing all the romantic bits —"

"Romance?" Jenny tripped on a cracked section of sidewalk. "There's no romance in softball."

"Uh-huh. Only because your dad's got a rulebook two miles long. Trust me, there's plenty of romance *if* you open up to your teammates enough to actually ask them about their lives. And I'm, err, not just talking about the girl-girl thing."

He squirmed at this and Jenny crossed her arms.

"I don't talk with my teammates simply because it's easier. I'm never actually around long enough to make friends."

Chuck ignored her, as he usually did when she turned up the attitude, and she had to actually walk faster to hear him. "Coach Laurie married an ex-baseball player whose kid was on the team. Needless to say the team just grew up with the girl and here they are now."

Most girls were in the dugout, pulling on cleats and smiling. Some shoved each other in a good-natured way Jenny had only seen on made-for-TV movies. You know, the kind of movies showing the perfect family life, showing what exactly a home was.

The movies where Jenny immediately changed the channel.

Even from here she could tell this wasn't a team filled with little, twelve year-old, whiny brats. She couldn't spot anyone who looked younger than fifteen. Most were tall, beefy, confident in their strides, their stances. The kind of team that'd take one look at Jenny and want nothing to do with her, with the threat of what she represented, the threat to their *position* on the team. Nothing got a team's hackles up more than someone who might steal their place.

She lifted the brim of her hat to see better. Practice clearly hadn't started yet, but she felt the excitement in the air, saw the girls laughing, enjoying themselves.

It was as if they wanted to be there.

As if they wanted to play softball.

Jenny looked away. She didn't want to see their happiness.

It was wrong, somehow, that they smiled and had fun while the teams she'd played on… well, the only time girls smiled was if someone made a mistake and made you look good.

Or maybe, maybe she didn't want to see their happiness because the second she stepped onto the field she'd upset that balance. Sam Taylor's daughter always did.

"They… they look happy."

Chuck nudged her with his shoulder. "Why do you think I insisted your dad get a place out here and not closer to the clubhouse?"

She smiled, or tried to.

That was Chuck for you. Always looking out for her.

The only problem was who'd be looking out for those girls? She highly doubted they were prepared for the 'Taylor Legacy' to invade their field.

Invade, and then leave just as quickly and silently as she'd came.

Instead of going to the bleachers filled with handfuls of nosy parents and fans, Chuck headed for right field. They stood there, Jenny listening to Chuck as he talked about the team, about how excited he was that she could play for a good, solid team.

But standing there, watching those girls laughing and having 'fun,' all she wanted was to turn around and never see them again.

Jenny clutched the fence, feeling the cool metal dig into her hands. She didn't want to be here. She'd change everything for them. She wouldn't mean to, but her name alone would be enough to start shifting the balance.

The competition would grow, intensify, and between one breath and the next, the smiles would be gone. Like a forgotten memory. And it'd be all her fault.

"I don't want to ruin this." Jenny gripped the metal fence, felt as the triangle shapes dug into her palms. "I'll ruin their happiness."

Chuck chewed on his bottom lip, glancing at her once and then back at the team. "You don't think it's cause you might be afraid? Afraid of smiling once in awhile?"

"I do smile."

"Smiling over Lucky Charms doesn't count." Chuck shook his head. "A girl like you shouldn't need a reason to smile. It should come as natural as breathing. These girls," he nodded at the field, "they'll be good for you."

She didn't like that Chuck was probably right. But it still didn't make it hurt any less.

"I'm not afraid." She wasn't. Far from it. "I just don't want to ruin a good thing."

"Maybe you should let those girls be the judge of that." He didn't wait for her to respond, just gave her a slap on the back and then wandered towards the bleachers.

Jenny stayed right where she was.

She felt trapped, closed in. First her dad with his stupid lipstick, Chuck always looking out for her, and finally this team.

She didn't want anything to do with them.

Jenny turned, ready to run to some obscure part of the park and to think and figure out some plan to get her life back.

She didn't get far.

Jenny smacked into the biggest, burliest chest she'd ever seen on a girl. Her head jerked back and she stumbled backwards into the fence, tripping on her sneakers. Somehow she managed to grab the fence, keeping herself from going down completely.

Oh, and that chest she smacked into?

It belonged to a girl nearly as tall as her dad, who was definitely on steroids, and whose scowl was so deep and crinkled Jenny was positive the girl's face was permanently stuck that way.

She also wore a softball hat and the T-shirt that said, "I KILLED THE LAST PITCHER WHO THREW AT ME."

The Giant crossed her arms, which further accented the 'KILLED' statement, and leaned closer to Jenny. "Who the hell are you?"

FIVE

The Giant stepped forward. One paw easily held her bat bag while the other was propped up on her hip. Definitely an intimidation stance.

Not like the girl needed it.

Jenny hung from her place on the fence, barely keeping herself upright, and tried to think of way out that didn't involve a black eye or two.

Nothing came up.

"I said, who the hell are you?"

This was also apparently a mean giant.

"Jenny."

"Fine. Jenny." The Giant bit out Jenny's name. "What the hell are you doing here?"

Okay. Now Jenny considered herself a fairly smart girl. She knew when to throw at batters, when to slide into home plate and aim for the catcher's kneecap, but she also knew when she was out-gunned.

This chick, here?

Oh, yeah. Jenny was definitely out-gunned.

She might be out-gunned, but she could handle her own. She'd faced more than her share of batters like the Giant and could put up a good fight. It'd be a dirty, hair-puller of a fight, and biting was definitely on the table, but when faced with a Giant weighing three times her size. Jenny couldn't exactly be chivalrous now could she?

Jenny straightened, using the fence to push off. What had she done to piss this girl off? Her dad in the papers? Did the Giant know who Jenny was? Had she heard about Sam Taylor's daughter joining Sunny View High?

Not a pleasant thought. She'd kill Jenny for sure.

"I asked you a question and you ain't answering," Giant said. "What are you doing here?"

"Well, I wasn't actually doing anything." It was true. She hadn't been doing *anything*.

"It looks like you were scouting my team." Giant's lip curled up. Her words tossed spit into the air which barely missed Jenny. "Where are you from? You from Mount Crest? Did they send you here to spy on us?"

"Spy?" Was this girl actually serious? "Umm… no. See, if I was going to spy I wouldn't have been walking the other way. As in *away* from the field. Not to mention I'd at least wait until practice actually *started* so I could watch you practice."

Giant's face contorted into some angry mixture of fury and bloating. Her bag slipped from her shoulder and hit the grass with a dull thunk.

Maybe sarcasm wasn't the best way to go with a girl who had such an obvious short fuse.

The Giant raised her meaty fist into the air.

The fence pressed into Jenny's back. She had no weapon, no bats to hit Giant's knees with. Ducking was her best bet. It was either that or taking the hit.

And like that, the thought gripped her.

If Jenny got into a fight, they wouldn't let her play. Not her mom. Not the school. Definitely not the coach.

She didn't move.

Instead, she squeezed her eyes closed and waited for the punch.

It didn't come.

Jenny peeked an eye open.

The Giant still stood there, face contorted in fury, but this time her anger wasn't directed at Jenny. Instead, it was directed at the guy holding the Giant's fist.

Standing nearly as tall as the giant, he didn't flinch or move as the Giant strained for freedom. With loose jeans, a mostly tucked-in and slightly wrinkled t-shirt, he wasn't shaking in his boots. If anything, he seemed more annoyed than afraid.

He also shouldn't look as good as he did for wearing a wrinkled t-shirt.

"Lacey," his voice, calm and soothing like an ocean breeze snaked down her neck. "We've talked about this."

Jenny shivered. She was pretty certain there was some rule in creation against someone having a voice that… that captivating. It *had* to be against the rules.

Her dad's rules for sure.

"I wasn't doing anything," Lacey growled.

"Really?" He glanced at Jenny and she caught a glimpse of opal blue eyes. "You weren't really going to pummel the transfer student on her first day?"

Jenny blinked. It took a moment to register what he'd said, mostly because with one look he'd made her breathing slightly more difficult.

Then, it clicked. New. Transfer. First day.

Just her luck the guy who'd saved her also figured out she was the new kid in town. And maybe, just maybe, he'd figured out whose daughter she was. When he let that little detail slip, Jenny highly doubted Lacey would be stopped a second time from beating the crap out of her.

Which would be a good thing for getting her off the team.

Still, this was turning into one hell of a day. And for a Sunday, that was saying a lot.

"What? New transfer student?" Lacey rounded on Jenny's saver, the soon to be first guy she avoided at all costs (in case he knew her secret, not because he was cute).

Lacey, by the way, wasn't a quiet person.

Jenny winced. In fact, she was fairly certain everyone in the park could hear.

"Jason," Lacey growled, "what the hell are you talking about?"

Jason. That was his name. A name that matched his face, intense and focused. Strong. Unbending. Of course, he had to be in order to hold back the Giant's fist, who even now strained against him.

The muscles in Lacey's arm bunched as she pulled. Still, her fist didn't move. He wasn't even straining.

"Are you going to hit her?" Jason asked.

"You gonna let me?"

"No."

"Then I won't. Promise."

Jenny wasn't buying it.

Neither, apparently, was Jason. He didn't let go of Lacey's paw.

And while Jenny didn't mind being rescued by Prince Charming, she was more than capable of standing on her own two feet.

Okay, normally she wasn't smashed against a fence and normally she didn't have some random, very cute guy jumping in to save her. She also didn't usually have the growing attention of the softball team.

Sure enough, the dugout was now empty of girls, girls who were now making their way over… and a few even had bats.

There was no batting practice in right field where Jenny was, unless she counted herself.

Which she didn't.

Shit.

SIX

J enny pushed away from the fence. "Umm…thanks, but I could have handled her."

Both Jason and Lacey looked at Jenny, eyebrows quirked up.

It was the same reaction, the same facial expression, and she put two and two together. They had to be brother and sister. And if she was a betting girl (which she wasn't), she was betting they were twins.

Lucky her.

One cute guy and one massive, angry giant.

"Is that right?" Lacey drawled. "You could have handled me?"

Jason, apparently deciding it was safe to unleash his sister, let go.

Lacey didn't charge.

That was definitely a good thing because right now, Jenny was trying hard to fake her tough-girl attitude.

"And what," Lacey asked, "were you planning to do? Fall down so I trip over you? Climb over the fence? Scream my ears off?"

"I'm a fast base runner."

Lacey's scowl deepened. Jason, on the other hand, smiled.

In truth, it was a smile that nearly knocked Jenny back into the fence. Add his smile to the list of rule-breaking against creation. No one, especially someone like him, should have *that* kind of smile. How was she supposed to not fall over?

"A base runner, huh?" Jason said. "I knew it. You came with Chuck, didn't you?"

"Chuck?" Both Lacey and Jenny said at the same time.

"Really?" Jason gave his sister a long look. "You're telling me you spotted her immediately, decided to kill her; but Chuck, who's been hanging around for the past month you didn't notice?"

"No."

"Unbelievable."

But he said this with a smile, a fond smile, as if he hadn't expected anything less. Then he turned that smile back to Jenny, and she had to grip the fence to keep herself upright.

"I'm Jason by the way, and this brute's my sister."

"I figured."

Jason held his hand out and after only a slight hesitation, Jenny shook it.

Sparks.

That was the only way to describe what she felt the second her fingers touched his. A spark so great she felt it to tip of her ponytail. A spark which zipped into her stomach.

But it didn't leave. Didn't fade or die away either.

Instead, it stayed there, smoldering and growing in intensity as she held Jason's hand.

There was a slight upturn of Jason's lips as if he knew exactly the kind of effect he had on her. Which was definitely not cool.

"Nice to meet you." Jenny stepped back and shoved her hand into her pocket. The spark in her hand disappeared.

The spark in her stomach?

Not so much.

"Aren't you going to tell me your name?" Jason asked.

Jenny blinked. She hadn't done that? "It's Jenny."

She tried to ignore the heat rolling across her face. Wasn't this just great? His first impression: saving her from his sister. His second: her blushing to death.

Lacey crossed her arms and glared at her brother. "Well, Jenny, the Jenny-whose-name-I'd-already-figured-out, you gonna tell me why you're here?"

"We've already covered that, Lace." Jason patted his sister on the arm. "She's here with Chuck."

"Right. Like I know who the hell Chuck is."

Jason turned to the field and pointed towards Chuck, who was now on the field and talking with a taller, older woman. Definitely the coach.

Jenny's stomach plummeted. She needed to convince Chuck this was absolutely the worst team for her. If Lacey was this protective about a strange girl watching practice, what would happen when she found out the truth?

Jenny wouldn't survive one practice.

When Lacey found out that Jenny transferred teams as easily as changing underwear, she'd kill her. She wouldn't let Jenny ruin the team.

Not to mention Jenny didn't *want* to do that; she didn't want to steal their smiles.

Jason gave Jenny another smile. "Chuck's been scouting the *Angels* and Sunny View's team for a month. I checked and he's not a scout, so I'm guessing he's with Jenny and she's the newest transfer student at Sunny View. Did I get that right?"

The spark in her stomach started sparking again.

"Umm… yeah. I am. Chuck's a…friend of the family." She needed to get out of here and fast.

She noticed the slight tightening in his jaw, the way he shifted his weight from one foot to the other. He had to know about her, about who she was.

Jenny tried to get a feel for Jason, but he was closed now. Like he'd suddenly distanced himself, dampened his smile.

She didn't blame him. After all, she was a threat—to someone on the team, anyway. Teams didn't like upstart transfer students who might snatch away their hard-earned spots.

Lacey hefted her bat bag from the grass and waved to the other girls. It was like an 'all clear' sign or something. The team paused, glanced between each other, then kept coming.

Jenny was screwed. Seriously screwed.

"What position do you play?" Lacey made the question sound casual, but Jenny knew better.

"She probably plays them all," Jason answered for her, but then he turned his attention to the whole team. "But I think you've got plenty of time to interrogate her later, *after* practice. Actually, aren't all of you late for practice?"

The whole *Angels* team had lined themselves in a semi-circle behind Jenny. The only thing standing between her and them was this flimsy fence.

And the only thing standing between her and Lacey (other than Jenny's fast feet), was Jason.

This definitely wasn't the way she wanted to start things out. Especially when she noticed all the smiles, all the laughter, was gone.

Suddenly it was too much. The move from San Diego. Her mom's tears when her dad hadn't come home. When he'd missed dinner.

The lipstick.

Softball.

A team that was already standing united against her, as if they knew she was poison, that she'd hurt someone, would steal someone's position.

They were a family. It was clear as day.

And it was clear Jenny wasn't welcome.

Not like she deserved to be. Not after what she'd do to them.

She couldn't be here. Couldn't hurt them the way she'd hurt all the others, like the way her dad repeatedly hurt her and her mom.

Jenny ran.

She swerved around Lacey, who hadn't expected Jenny's sudden movement, which caused her to knock back into her brother.

Jenny's ball cap lifted off her head. It thumped once against her back, ponytail holding it in place, then it was gone. She didn't stop.

She ran towards Chuck, who stood on the field, chatting with a woman in softball shorts and cleats. The woman had an easy, relaxed stance. Confident, reassured. In one look, Jenny knew this woman was Coach Laurie and that she was everything Jenny wasn't.

So was the girl standing beside her, a girl who looked about Lacey's age.

Jenny saw all this in a split-second as she wiped her watering eyes before her tears fell.

"Jenny!" Chuck turned, hearing her sneakers on the dirt. "I'd like you to meet Laurie. Did you know she used to play for —"

"I need to leave."

"Jenny? What is it?"

Both women were looking at her.

Jenny didn't want them to see her like this… hell she didn't even like Chuck seeing her like this. "I just…can we just go? Please?"

Chuck's lips pressed into a tight line. He nodded. "Sure. Let's get you home."

She didn't hear what else he said because she was already running for the truck. And once she was away from everyone, she let the tears come.

She knelt beside Chuck's truck, its solid body separating her from the softball team who already hated her. A team whose smiles she'd already stolen.

There was a crunch of Chuck's shoes on the gravel, and then he was there beside her. "It didn't go well?"

She couldn't answer. Couldn't speak because her throat was suddenly so tight and it was hard to breathe.

Lacey had taken one look at her and had known immediately Jenny was a threat. Just like she always was. To someone.

It wasn't until Chuck got her in the car, with the silent ride back home and finally pulling into the driveway, that she found her voice again. Oh the tears were still there, still kept pouring out of her eyes like a leaking faucet. She couldn't turn them off, but alone with Chuck it didn't really matter.

He'd seen her cry more times than anyone else.

She wiped at her eyes with her t-shirt. "Is it worth it? Is me playing softball worth…worth hurting all these people?"

Chuck turned off the engine. "How have you hurt anyone? Seems to be me you're the one upset."

"They're a family, Chuck. A *family*. When I transfer to another school, after I rip away someone's starting spot—a spot they worked hard to earn—I don't just hurt that one person. I hurt everyone."

Chuck pulled off his ball cap and scratched his head. They sat in silence for several long minutes before Chuck sighed and let the hat fall into his lap.

"I don't know, Jenny. I'd say playing softball is worth it for most people, but…"

"But for me it's different."

And it was. Most people weren't carrying a famous baseball name, weren't pushed into a sport because it was what their dad wanted. Most people didn't have personal coaches.

"I will say this, though." Chuck reached across her lap and squeezed her hand. "I think you'll do all right here. I wish I could have brought you here sooner. Wish you'd played for a team like the *Angels* when you were younger. You would have had fun. But it's not too late, you know. You can still have fun."

She saw the garage door open and a smoky-black sports car back out, the engine gunning as if it couldn't wait to tear out of there. Her dad, with the convertible top down, spotted them and immediately shut off the engine.

Chuck's hand tightened on hers, then he pulled away. "I meant what I said, Jenny. You can still have fun."

"Tell that to my dad." She got out and slammed the door behind her. Her eyes were red and puffy and she looked like hell.

He probably wouldn't notice. He never did.

At the end of the day, she didn't matter. At the end of the day this was her dad's life, his future legacy, as if she owed him for not being a boy. A boy he'd wanted. A boy he'd bought the most expensive champagne to celebrate with his team when she was born. A boy to carry on his baseball legacy.

Instead, he got Jenny.

SEVEN

Jenny stared at her dad with his new black shades reflecting the late morning sunlight, even now moving like he was on the field. Steps light, slight bounce on the balls of his feet. He was always ready for the next fly ball.

He was also always ready with the charm, which he turned on now, full-blast. Jenny glanced behind her at the driveway. No reporters.

That meant her dad wanted something.

The talk. That's right. With all the 'excitement' at the field she'd forgotten.

She felt like throwing up. Maybe if she threw up her cereal all over his expensive, hot-date shoes he'd forget about the talk.

He was there in two long strides, picked her up and swung her into a hug, the kind he'd only given when she was small. It made her even queasier. Unfortunately. he ended the swinging before she got a good gag reflex going.

She hung there, limp in his arms, waiting for him to let go.

His smile, dazzling and handsome as always, fell an inch. Then the moment passed and he had his game face on. He let her go and turned to Chuck, shaking the older man's hand.

"Chuck. Good to see you. How'd the pitching practice go? Jenny making headway on her knuckle ball?"

Jenny bit her tongue to keep from saying anything. Like she already had seven different pitches at different speeds. Gee, maybe she should work on those and make them awesome?

But no. Her dad wanted to see the numbers.

Wanted to tell everyone just how many pitches Jenny had, regardless if they were reliable pitches or not.

"She'll get there. These things take time. Not to mention she's still growing." Chuck lifted his free hand. "Her hand isn't quite big enough to do the trick. Anyway, this morning Jenny had a great idea about meeting her future teammates. We just got back from the field."

"Oh, is that right?" Her dad glanced at Jenny. "And how'd that go?"

"Actually…."

This was it. Her chance to ask about switching schools, telling him she wouldn't fit in. She could do this. "I'm not sure, about the team, I mean."

Chuck's eyebrows rose in surprise. "Why's that, Jenny?"

"They just seemed really tight. Like a family and I think me coming in and then leaving again —"

Her dad jumped in. "I'll bet you had everyone lining up to get your autograph? Or," he chuckled, "asking for mine?"

Jenny dug her fingers into her palms. He hadn't listened at all. "No."

"No?" His eyebrows lifted. "Well, why not? How are we supposed to tell the press about you being the newest starter if no one actually knows?"

She thought about Jason, about how he seemed to know, but how instead of saying anything had protected Jenny. He'd protected her from not only Lacey but the whole team.

"It didn't come up," she said.

He frowned, clearly not pleased. "I'm disappointed. That's what I pay you for, Chuck. You're supposed to make my little girl look like a superstar out there."

Chuck's hand landed on Jenny's shoulder and he gave her a firm pat. "Trust me. She does."

Her dad snorted. Of course, all good things must only come from the Taylor name.

"Besides," Chuck went on, "Change is hard for most people, Jenny included. She's right, Sam. They're a close knit team. They've been playing together since they were twelve. Some things you can't rush and some things are just left quietly to the side until the right time comes up."

"Left to the side?" his voice was biting and sharp.

Chuck kept his gaze on her dad. "It's not an easy thing to be, Sam, being your daughter. Jenny's gonna have enough problems getting the team to open up to her. No point adding insult to injury with her knocking some starter out of the rotation."

"There's always more teams," her dad hissed.

Now it was Jenny's turn to jump in. "That's right! There *are* more teams, Chuck."

"Yeah, but not like this one," Chuck told them. "After all, your instructions were clear: find the best team for Jenny. Well? These guys are the best. Of course, it's your call."

Jenny glanced back and forth between them, her heart pounding. Would her dad listen to Chuck? Would he let her go on another team?

The two men couldn't be more different. Chuck in his flannels and dirt-dusted jeans. Her dad in his perfect, immaculate suit, looking exactly like his celebrity pictures, the ones girls taped to their walls.

"I suppose you're right." Her dad glanced at his gold watch (with real diamonds in the face too). "I don't have much time, but you know these teams better than I do, Chuck. I'll take your word on it."

Jenny's felt like she was falling.

He smiled at her. "I'm glad it went well, Jenny."

But it didn't!

She knew that look, the distraction in his eyes. He was already thinking about his next hot date, about the girls he'd have all over him and the guys he'd be drinking with.

It didn't matter what she said, not now. He'd made his decision. She was stuck.

"Listen, I'm glad I caught you both. I wanted to give you this last night, Jen, but you know. Meeting and all that." He wrapped a hand around her shoulder and steered her to his new car—she had no idea what the hell kind of car it was, only that it was shiny, black, and the second car purchase this year.

"I wanted this to be a surprise for you and now's as good a time as any, right?"

He wasn't talking about the car. Not like she was surprised.

Instead, he reached into the open top and pulled out a bat from the backseat. The sleek, black color shimmered in the sunlight, dark and menacing. A softball bat. The words 'Louisville Slugger' etched in silver along the barrel.

It was the same brand of bat she already used, but hers was simple. Ordinary. Not flashy or shiny.

"Uh, what is it?" Jenny asked. "I mean, besides a bat."

"Your surprise." Her dad grinned and he held it out to her. "Go on. Give it a swing."

She didn't want to, but again she had no choice. She swung the bat. Once. It was light and perfectly balanced. A bat that felt like money.

But not perfect for her.

A softball bat was something you were meant to you know, hit *soft-balls* with. This was the kind of bat that should be framed and hung over the fireplace or something, like really expensive jewelry you wouldn't actually wear for fear of losing it.

She held the expensive toy back to him.

"Well?" He asked, voice eager. "What do you think? Think you can hit balls into the green with this?"

"How should I know? I haven't actually tried to hit with it."

Her dad's charm dropped a notch, obviously not expecting her attitude. Well, if he was around more he'd see it on a more regular occasion.

Chuck stepped in, even as Jenny crossed her arms and glared at her father. "I've heard some rumors. The Lightning brand, isn't it?"

Rumors? Over a softball bat?

"Chuck got it right in one shot," her dad said, not to be outdone. This was *his* surprise after all. "Just like I thought he would."

"It's Louisville's new prototype." He handed the bat to Chuck, who gave it a much more careful look-over than Jenny had.

Chuck stepped back and gave it a slow test swing, then a faster one.

"When I heard about it, hell, I just had to give them a call and get one for you Jen." Her dad went on and told her how it was the newest in softball bat technology, about the 'core' in the barrel, how it had been lengthened to really take advantage of the sweet spot and blah, blah, blah.

He retrieved the bat from Chuck, held it easily in his hands, and swung it back and forth as if he could imbed his magic into it for her.

She didn't want the bat.

She didn't want his magic.

"This," her dad said, "*this* is the kind of bat professional athletes use. *This* bat will see you to the championship game this year. *This* bat will knock you into all kinds of world records and into professional ball."

Her breath whooshed out of her. "Professional ball?"

Jenny's head spun. She sucked in a mouthful of air. She could barely hear her words over her thundering heart. "What are you talking about? Everyone *knows* there's no professional women's softball."

Okay. Technically there was, but right now they didn't exactly have the kind of career girls dreamed of having. It wasn't like baseball, not like the Major League. Softball, the whole four teams who played three months out of the year, wasn't even a blip on the radar.

Her dad though, just smiled.

"Oh, it's there, Jen. Right there for you and your future. If anyone is going to see professional softball take off, it'll be you."

Future? Hers?

"Me?"

She didn't dare breathe. Didn't dare blink. He had to be joking. This had to be… had to be something else because there was no way, no freakin' way she was going to let her dad plan her future.

Not when her future was the one thing that was hers.

The one that thing that was *Jenny's*.

"That's right." Her dad hugged her again. The smell of spicy cologne made her gag, but he didn't let go. "Sam Taylor's daughter. If anyone's going to make it happen, if anyone's going to bring in serious sponsorships and propel pro women's softball forward, it's you."

EIGHT

J enny did the only thing she could. She locked herself in her room.

Not like it mattered. Not when her dad had taken off and had no idea she was upset.

Her mom and Chuck, on the other hand, did know.

"I don't understand, Chuck," her mom whispered just outside her door. "I thought she'd be happy. Her father wants what's best for her."

"I know, Carol. But maybe Jenny should figure out what's best for her."

"He's her father! He talks with her, wants to see her and spend time with her...." Her mom's voice trailed off. "No, that isn't fair to her."

"Everything about this is hard on you and on Jenny. Give her time. She'll talk when she's ready and you'll work it out."

Jenny left the door and curled up on her bed.

Chuck had successfully calmed her mom down without actually answering any of her questions. Maybe that was for the best.

"After all, that's how this family works. If there's a problem you don't talk about it."

She *didn't* want to talk about it.

But not talking didn't change anything. She was still going to Sunny View and she would still play for their team.

Jenny pulled at her ponytail. Being underage and still very much in her parents' control meant there was actually very little Jenny could do. Except she could find information about the *Angels* and the Sunny View softball team.

Knowledge was power, right? And that's why the internet was invented. Maybe just knowing more about the team and about the girls would help prepare her… for what, she didn't know.

Running away, maybe?

Jenny booted up her computer (first box unpacked of course) and got to work. The first article that popped up was about Elizabeth Evans, who hurt her arm a couple months before. The injury wasn't what caught her attention, that made her sit up straighter and not dare move.

Elizabeth was the daughter of ex-pro baseball player Jack Evans.

Someone else like her? Someone who'd grown up with a dad who played professional ball?

Jenny read further, skimming the article as fast as her eyes let her. No. Elizabeth wasn't like her. Elizabeth's dad had quit baseball when she was still young, had given up baseball to be a father.

Her hand tightened on the mouse and snapped the web page closed.

This was a tight group of girls, and they'd stomp her into the ground if she displaced even one person on the team. It didn't matter that they *needed* Jenny's arm or her bat to meet Mount Crest for the Championship title.

The coach might want Jenny. But the team wouldn't.

Jenny dropped her head onto the keyboard, making the keys go crazy and her computer beep in annoyance.

"There has to be a way out of this."

So far, she hadn't a clue what 'this' was. And even when Monday morning came, with her usual stomach knots at starting a new school, she was nowhere closer to an answer.

Jenny stared at the Sunny View campus, backpack slung over her shoulder, her jean jacket doing nothing to keep out the morning chill.

She scuffed her boots into the cement and tried to ignore the curious glances as other students vacated vans, SUVs, and hot red little cars, as they eyed the new girl.

The new girl whose own eyes were rimmed with dark lines from lack of sleep.

Meeting your future softball team (who hated you) and then learning your dad had planned out your future made sleep about as impossible as zipping away to Never Never Land and never growing up.

Sunny View looked like every other campus, which actually meant they looked nothing alike. Every school layout was different, every building either named after a dead guy or someone who donated a shit ton of money.

And let's not forget every building had rooms organized by numbers. But what each building was actually for, which classes would be where, required a personal tour of the campus.

About the only thing decently easy to find (after going into the wrong building) was the Administration Building, and like all Administration Buildings, there was the just-past-middle-age woman manning the front desk, currently on the phone. She wasn't a secretary, of course (those titles weren't allowed anymore), but she was thin and her hair had turned a nice silvery color.

She smiled at Jenny and motioned she'd just be a minute. Jenny rocked on her heels and tried to blend in, not drawing attention to herself. A couple students came in, dropped some yellow paper in a slot, and left. One or two eyed her, but for the most part Jenny succeeded in being wallpaper. They didn't stop or stare, didn't ask who she was.

The one plus to waiting here, pretending not to be noticed, was the bowl of candy on the woman's desk. Candy, which Jenny just happened to have a perfect birds-eye-view of inside the bowl.

And Jenny, like any new (and slightly nervous, ready to throw up) student, peeked inside to see if there was something that would settle her nerves.

Taffy?

Chewy candy was about the last thing she needed right now, not to mention it always made her mouth water and drool in a disgusting fashion.

Then again…

She reached in and grabbed two pieces. It wasn't like she was here to make friends. Who cared if she drooled a little? She was here to go to school and hopefully, get out of playing softball.

The glass entrance door opened, but since Jenny currently had her hand in the candy bowl, she didn't actually register someone had come in…and hadn't gone back out.

"Hi," a girl's voice said behind her. "I recommend the strawberry melon one. It's my favorite."

Jenny jerked her hand out and nearly knocked over the candy bowl. She glanced over her shoulder and her stomach hit bottom.

It was Elizabeth. The girl whose father used to play pro baseball, too.

Not that Elizabeth was a girl. Far from it. The way she carried herself, books propped up on one hip, a smile that was as warm and friendly as Lacey's wasn't, there was no mistaking she was a senior.

A senior on the softball team who probably thought Jenny was out to steal her spot.

Of course, that didn't explain the smile.

"Good morning, Elizabeth." Mrs. Crowley, the not-secretary, hung up the phone. "Did you come in with Laurie today?"

Laurie?

Who was…but then Jenny remembered her conversation with Chuck and his mention of romance. Laurie had been the coach of the *Angels.* Was she a teacher here too? Oh, please don't let her be the softball coach. Right now that was the very last thing Jenny needed.

"I did. Dad's all worked up about college teams. Laurie practically yanked me into the car this morning to get me away from him."

Mrs. Crowley clucked. "Your dad's always worked up, but we've got you for another season and that's what matters."

"If my arm's better." Elizabeth tucked a strand of hair behind her ears, still holding herself cool and relaxed.

"It will be, dear. You'll see."

Elizabeth glanced back to Jenny. Her smile was still there.

This didn't make sense. Why was she smiling? Jenny was a pitcher, just like Lacey and Elizabeth. Jenny being here meant less pitching time for them!

"Anyway," Elizabeth said, "I just saw Jenny and wanted to say hi."

"Oh!" Mrs. Crowley beamed. "I hadn't realized you knew Jenny."

Jenny's mouth fell open. "We, uh, don't."

But Elizabeth was waving away her comment like it was an annoying breeze. "We met yesterday. Briefly. Have you gotten her class schedule? If you like I can give her the tour."

Mrs. Crowley insisted this wasn't necessary, but Elizabeth simply did that waving thing again and Mrs. Crowley handed over the paperwork. Elizabeth swiped two candies from the jar, both pink, and told Mrs. Crowley to not work too hard.

Trapped. There was no way out of Elizabeth's clutches.

A student rolled up to the glass doors in a wheel chair. Head bent forward, back hunched, he seemed like any ordinary guy except for the wheel chair—and the piercing glare as Jenny opened the door for him.

He jerked forward on his wheels and Jenny jumped back before he ran over her toes. "Did it look like I needed your damn help?"

Elizabeth crossed her arms. "Morning to you, too, Dan. Just as cheerful as always?"

His face twisted into a smile. "Elizabeth. Aren't you just as sunny as ever?"

Jenny could tell Elizabeth wanted to say something, wanted to snap back some reply, but somehow managed to swallow her words and then, to Jenny's surprise, beamed a smile back at Jenny. It was like she flipped a switch and the sunshine was back.

Dan grunted in response, as if this just provided his point.

"Come on, Jenny. Let's give you that tour." And then she shooed Jenny out the door, leaving Mrs. Crowley to deal with the very unhappy Dan. Jenny didn't know who was worse. Dan and his rain-clouds or Elizabeth and her sunshine.

"Don't worry about him," Elizabeth mumbled. "He's always like that. Anyways, I wanted to apologize for what happened yesterday."

"Apologize?"

"That's right. For Lacey. She shouldn't have acted that way. And neither should the team. Here, let me see your schedule."

She slipped the paper from Jenny's numb fingers. "Okay. We'll start with the D Building."

'D' of course didn't actually stand for anything and Jenny sighed as her head spun after two minutes of the tour.

Elizabeth laughed at her confusion. "I promise, you'll get used to it."

"I doubt I'll be here that long."

Elizabeth looked at her funny. The happy girl faded into someone else, someone who knew exactly what Jenny was saying and why.

A couple of students jostled them as they stood there, blocking the paved path between 'D' Building and 'Carter' Building. Jenny stepped to the side, letting them pass.

"I get it, you know," Elizabeth said. "I mean, not completely since Dad quit when I was young, but I get it. I know what my life would have been like."

"So. You know. Who I am, who my dad is."

Elizabeth nodded. She held out Jenny's schedule. "Laurie told me after you left. The others, they don't know, but I wanted to meet you first, to tell you I understand."

Jenny glanced at the schedule, and after a second, took it. "You don't understand. You don't because your dad loved you enough to give it up."

"Yeah," Elizabeth whispered. "I know."

Unlike Jenny's dad.

They stood there, staring at each other with the stream of students continuing to move past them, to carry on with their normal lives, with friends and boyfriends, with all-day and night texting.

Students who had no idea what it was like growing up with a famous father. A famous father who played baseball.

"Do you…" Jenny looked away.

She didn't want to see Elizabeth's sympathy, didn't want to know there truly was one person here who understood. One person who could be her friend. If Jenny let her.

"Do you know where my homeroom is? I think I can probably find the rest…" Jenny caught sight of a familiar, tall shape with his wavy, dark brown hair and easy smile. A shape, she realized, slowly making his way towards them.

Jason.

Her luck truly couldn't be this bad.

NINE

J enny sucked in a breath.

Jason looked the same as yesterday, still smiling, still relaxed and confident. This time, though, instead of being surrounded by the softball team (thank God!), he was surrounded by a handful of guys —all wearing baseball hats.

They laughed with Jason and one gave him a knuckle slap on the shoulder of his letterman jacket. He was on the baseball team?

Jason knocked his buddy back and the movement caused him to look in Jenny's direction. His eyes widened and the smile died from his lips.

Jenny didn't think. She grabbed Elizabeth's hand and yanked the senior into the nearest bathroom. She nearly trampled over two chatty freshman who had re-applied their completely unnecessary lipstick and were talking about some stupid dance coming up.

Jenny swung the door shut and flipped the lock on the inside.

Elizabeth stood there, books against her chest, a half-smile plastered on her face. "You mind telling me why we're hiding in the bathroom?"

"We're not."

"Uh-huh."

Jenny double-checked the lock. Yep. Still locked. She hoped Jason hadn't actually seen her…but if he had?

Her face paled.

Oh, God. He could be waiting outside the bathroom right now!

But that was stupid. Why would he do that? She was no one. "First Elizabeth, now Jason," Jenny muttered to herself. "And the bell hasn't even rung."

"Are you sure we're not hiding in the bathroom?"

"Positive."

Jenny pressed her ear against the door, but the only thing she heard was the hum of student voices. She couldn't pick out Jason's voice. Not that she would know what his voice sounded like. Or that she even remembered what it sounded like. As if.

Elizabeth dropped her books onto the sink counter and crossed her arms. "So you didn't just hide in here because you spotted Jason Richards?"

"No. Of course not. Why would I do that?"

"Because he's extremely good looking. Single. And he has one hell of a smile."

"I hadn't noticed."

"Really?" Elizabeth's smile widened. "So you wouldn't care that yesterday he was actually pretty worried, you know, after you ran off?"

"He was?" The words sort of blurted out on their own. Shit.

"Maybe." Elizabeth flipped her hair over her shoulder and reclaimed her books. "Not that you care or anything, right? And because you don't care you won't mind if we leave the bathroom? I mean, you wouldn't want to be late on your first day."

Jenny winced. Okay, put like that her plan wasn't so hot. Not that she had a plan. Because she didn't.

"No, I umm…I don't care."

To prove her point, Jenny unlocked the door. See? She didn't care.

Of course, the way her palms were doused in sweat wasn't helping to prove anything. At least Elizabeth couldn't see how sweaty they were. She hoped.

Jenny stepped aside, indicating Elizabeth should go first (for politeness sake, not because Jason might be waiting), but Elizabeth didn't move past her. Instead, she tilted her head to the side, letting her gorgeous hair fall to her shoulders.

She had to be like the beauty queen on the team or something, but underneath that pretty face Jenny could see something…that kind of ruthless intensity you found only on the softball field.

She had no doubt Elizabeth had taken out her fair share of catchers when sliding into home. Even now, not being able to pitch because of her arm, Elizabeth looked more real, more human. She wasn't just this strange figment of Jenny's imagination that was actually being nice to her.

But that look in Elizabeth's eye…she *did* know what Jenny was going through. Not only that, she didn't resent Jenny for being here, for stepping up to pitch when Elizabeth herself couldn't.

For a brief moment, so brief it nearly knocked her over, she wanted to tell Elizabeth what her father had said about playing pro softball. Wanted to tell her about the lipstick, about her worries, about how playing softball had lost its spark.

Jenny shoved the thought aside. She didn't want to make friends. She was doing just fine on her own.

She crossed her arms. "What? Do I have something on my face?"

"I just wanted to know why," Elizabeth said. "Why were you surprised to see Jason?"

"No reason. I just, I just wasn't expecting to see him."

Jenny didn't wait for Elizabeth to try any more psychological insights into her pathetic life. She left the bathroom first, took two steps and came face to face with Jason.

Jason, who had definitely seen her, and who had definitely been waiting by the door for Jenny to come out.

The guys she'd seen him with were gone and it was like the halls themselves emptied leaving just the two of them. Jenny's mouth worked, trying to get words out… or maybe just trying to breathe. It was hard to tell.

Jason stood there in his letterman jacket and a green shirt—a green that really brought out the deep blue of his eyes. She didn't know what to say, not when Jason was smiling at her, making her stomach do all these strange things.

Her pulse quickened like she was on the mound facing one of the league's heaviest hitters.

"You okay?" he asked. "I saw you duck into the bathroom. I hope you weren't going to be sick or something."

Oh, God…he had seen her. And more importantly, he probably knew *why* she'd ran into the bathroom.

Jenny was saved from replying because time kicked back to normal and students refilled the halls.

Elizabeth sauntered out of the bathroom, her books once again propped up on her hip. "Jenny was hiding in the bathroom."

Jenny about fell over as she whirled at Elizabeth. "I was not!"

But Elizabeth simply grinned and gave Jenny a little nudge with her shoulder. "Jason, you know I think you scared her yesterday. You *always* have that effect on people."

Jason laughed. His laugh took Jenny by surprise. Deep and warm, as if he didn't have a care in the world. He probably didn't. He probably had a wonderful and supportive father. The kind of father who took the time to teach him baseball.

"Scared of me? Hardly. That would be my sister. The one who was trying to pummel her into right field."

"I imagine Jenny isn't used to seeing chivalry in the flesh." Elizabeth wrapped her arms around Jenny's shoulder and squeezed.

Jenny stood there frozen, trying to think of a way out of this terribly embarrassing situation.

But Elizabeth didn't stop there.

Oh, no. She had to go and make Jenny's day that much worse.

"Jason, your homeroom's right across from Jenny's. Why don't you show her the way? I need to talk to Laurie before the bell rings."

"Sure thing."

No. Not a sure thing. Not okay.

"Really," Jenny tried, "it's no big deal."

Jason shook his head. "Seriously. I insist. It's the least I could do after how my sister acted."

At least he didn't hold out his hand and expect her to take it.

Elizabeth gave Jenny's arm another squeeze, then slipped a strawberry taffy into her hand. "Have fun. Call me if you need anything. I mean it."

Then Elizabeth disappeared down the halls. The girl practically skipped with happiness, which didn't make a whole lot of sense since she was *injured*. Most girls in Elizabeth's situation would be fighting an uphill battle to convince colleges to give them a chance.

That was all fine and great for Elizabeth, but what Jenny didn't need was Elizabeth pushing her towards Jason. She didn't need a damn friend.

Jenny shoved her backpack higher up on her shoulder. "I can find my way, thanks."

"I know, but this gives me a chance to talk with you."

She ignored the way her stomach flipped.

She also didn't need Jason talking to her—or reminding her of the terrible disaster of yesterday's practice.

Jenny spotted a trashcan by the bathroom, was ready to toss the taffy into it, but then paused. It had been a nice gesture, even if Jenny didn't need her help.

She dropped it into her pocket. Jason noticed, but didn't say anything.

The saying nothing was good. All she had to do was keep her head down, keep any conversation to one word answers, and she'd survive. Right?

Well, it was a good plan.

At least until Jason tugged a Charger baseball cap from his backpack. The same hat Jenny had lost at the park.

"I believe," he held it out to her, "this is yours."

TEN

J enny stared at the hat as if it was going to bite her.

She didn't want it. Didn't want to think what this meant, that Jason had found it and tucked it away, keeping it safe until he saw her again. Like he knew he *would* see her again.

She definitely didn't want to think about what that meant.

He was supposed to hate her. He knew she was Sam Taylor's daughter, she just knew it! So why was he being so nice? And why the hell was he still standing there waiting for her to take the damn hat she clearly didn't want?

Jason held the hat up higher. "I promise, it's not going to bite."

Yes. It was. Because *he* had touched it.

"I saw it fall off yesterday. I wanted to return it."

He clearly wasn't going to stop until she took it. Fine.

Jenny snatched the hat from him and tried to keep her fingers to herself, tried to only touch the part he wasn't touching. As if it was that easy.

The second her fingers brushed his, she felt the same spark from yesterday. Felt it snake through her like it was a living, breathing thing.

She shoved the hat into her backpack, not even bothering to zip it closed. "Thanks."

Jenny spun on the heels of her boots, her attention fully focused on the students in front of her. She had no idea where she was going and didn't much care either. She just needed to get away from Jason and his kindness—kindness she definitely didn't deserve.

Jason, however, couldn't take a hint.

Or didn't want to.

He kept pace with her and he still wore his same grin, as if he knew why she was stomping away from him.

"You're welcome," he said, "for returning your hat."

She nodded.

There! All she had to do was make vague head motions. She was good at that. She did that to her mom all the time.

"You a baseball fan?"

She shook her head.

"Is your dad?"

She nodded.

"I guess he'd have to be."

And here it came. The moment she'd waited for.

Jenny stopped and faced Jason, letting her feet slide out into a ready stance, perfectly balanced, always at the ready. "Why are you asking me if you already know the answer?"

Jason gave an easy roll of his shoulders. "Just curious why you hadn't mentioned him yet."

"I'd say that's pretty obvious."

"What's obvious is you doing everything in your power to push me and Elizabeth away."

"If it's so obvious why are you still following me?"

Jenny flipped her ponytail at him and pushed open a set of double doors, entering an attached school building. The halls here looked the same as any other school hallway. The puke-orange colored lockers, complete with dents and worn handles, the students milling around on the faded, carpeted floor and the unused drinking fountains.

Right now, no one cared who she was.

Soon, however, they would care—along with everyone trying to be her friend. Some would want her dad's autograph while others would want some favor.

Everyone wanted *something* from her, just like everyone had an agenda.

Jason too. He wanted something.

Jason jogged to catch up with her. Even his breath came out in easy, controlled movements. "Look. I didn't mean to make you mad and I really did want to apologize for yesterday."

"Don't."

But still, Jason wouldn't take the hint. He slid in front of her and Jenny dug her boots into the carpet to keep from crashing into him. Which she totally didn't want to do. No more touching Jason. No more sparks.

The last thing she needed was sparks.

"And why not?" he asked. "Why can't I apologize? Why shouldn't I be nice to you?"

"Because I'm going to do everything your sister's team is afraid of me doing, okay? They weren't wrong to hate me. Now. Which is my homeroom?"

Jason's smile vanished.

Good. She needed him to back off. Needed to find some way out of this, of being in this school and on this team, and she couldn't do that when he was around.

She just couldn't think when he was around, not when he was smiling at her.

Jason pointed to the room on her right, which had an open door and the numbers '202' written above it. "Your homeroom. Mine's across the hall."

"Thanks."

Wasn't this just great? Now everyday she'd have to dodge Jason and hope he wasn't waiting for her. Which he shouldn't be doing.

Like right now.

She'd just told him to back off, had acted rude to him, and yet he was still standing there, rocking on his heels, waiting for her to say something.

It made her mad.

Mad he was trying to play nice, probably trying to find out some secret so he could pass it onto his sister, to try and save someone's starting spot from being snatched away.

There was no way, absolutely no way he was actually being nice to her—like he cared about her or something stupid like that.

Tired of no one being honest with her…Jenny just couldn't stand it. Not after what her dad said yesterday about her future and professional ball.

She just needed the truth. But the only person she could demand that truth from was Jason. She didn't know why. She just knew if she asked him, he'd tell her.

"Look," she snapped, "I don't know what you want or why you're here. So why don't you just tell me already so you can leave me alone?"

"I thought that was pretty obvious. I was walking you to homeroom."

"Which seniors don't do for sophomores."

"You're new. It'd have been rude not to."

Jenny dropped her bag and cocked her hip to the side. "I'm not moving until you tell me the truth."

"Even if you're late and get detention?"

"Wouldn't be the first time."

He shrugged. "You're a ballplayer. That's why."

She was about to ask if he did this with all the new softball players, but he beat her too it.

"I can tell," he said. "It's just something about you—and no, it's not because you mentioned being a fast base runner. It's the way you stand. See?"

Jenny glanced down.

Her hand slid off her hip. He was right. She was standing there with her feet spread, knees slightly bent…like she really was a ballplayer. This wasn't what she'd expected—and definitely not what she expected him to say.

"I've got a sense for people," Jason went on. "I got a sense for whether or not they're great players. And the great ones, let's just say they have a certain spark to them."

A spark?

Jenny tried not to think about the spark currently doing numbers on her insides, but she was pretty sure *that* wasn't what Jason was talking about.

"Well, how do you know? Just because you watch your sister play doesn't mean anything." She pointed to his letterman jacket. "Unless, of course, you play? Baseball?"

The openness in Jason changed. It was as if he pulled back from her or suddenly drew those horrible floral curtains closed and now blocked out the sun.

Only a tiny sliver of sunlight slipped through.

"I watch the softball team. They're good. They've got good players." He looked away and it felt like there was something he wasn't saying. "You'll fit right in—not only because you're a ballplayer, but I'm guessing you're a damn good one too."

For a second, Jenny was distracted by Jason closing off to her, and then what he said kicked in.

He thought she was a damn good player.

Just like her dad thought she was. No, that he believed in. Believed in enough to start talking about his future plans of her playing professional ball.

Jenny's chest tightened.

Her father was wrong about her.

Jason was wrong about her.

She wasn't a ballplayer. If Jason was right, if her father was right, then nothing she did mattered. She would be a ballplayer. Even if that was no longer her dream.

All she wanted to be was Jenny.

"Well, you're wrong." Jenny grabbed her backpack. "I'm not a 'damn good one.' I'm average and I do my part to help the team."

Jenny shoved past Jason and into her homeroom, completely

ignoring the stares from the half dozen students already sitting in their desks. She spotted a vacant desk in the corner, the one which felt like miles away from all the others and headed there.

One girl stuck her foot out right as Jenny passed. She easily skipped over it and caught her backpack before it slipped to the floor. Jenny glimpsed the girl's high ponytail, a nose too small for her face, and death glare that was becoming rather common. That's when she noticed the softball hat on her desk.

Great. Another Jenny fan. One she'd have to see—and avoid— every damn morning.

No one said anything about the attempted tripping. No one introduced themselves or offered to help.

This was fine.

It was better this way, better to sit on the outskirts, not really part of the school and yet forced to attend all the same. If only she wasn't forced to play softball too.

Jenny sank into the desk, grateful to have something normal and familiar underneath her. Normal was also figuring out where her next class was and how to further avoid the softball player in homeroom who hated her.

This was yet another thing she could handle. One she didn't need friends for.

Part of her expected Jason to still be there, hands tucked in his jean pockets with that knowing smile pulling at his lips.

But he wasn't there.

And that was okay.

Whenever anyone, guys included, expressed interest in getting to know her, she shut them down. She had to. It was better this way, better because then her dad didn't need to invoke rule number 683 about boys and Jenny's social life (which was silly since her social life included reading books and watching streaming movies on the internet).

However, what wasn't normal was the disappointment. The disappointment that Jason wasn't standing there, smiling at her.

No matter how hard she tried to convince herself this was completely silly… the disappointment didn't go away.

She wanted him to be standing there, waiting for her.

ELEVEN

The thing about schools is no rumor-mill in the world works faster. Throw in things like Twitter and Facebook and by the end of second period, the whole damn school knew about the newest transfer student on campus.

Jenny tucked her iPhone into her pocket as she trudged through the halls. At least no one had figured out the little detail about Jenny being Sam Taylor's daughter.

Give it a day. Two at most. And then… and then her status as being the new girl would change to the 'popular' girl.

She ignored the cafeteria's line and headed outside. Space and sunshine. That's what she needed right now.

Students overflowed on the green grass and walkways and Jenny stood there, studying the groups—the ones with their noses in books who ate a sandwich in one hand and turned the page with the other. There were also the students with the dreadlocks, the dark clothed Goths, and the nerds with their handheld video games and strategy guides.

And here she was, fully expected to once again navigate these treacherous waters.

If she approached the beautiful group (yes, boys and girls could be beautiful), she would be booted on her ass and wonderfully humiliated (while providing entertainment for the rest of the student body).

Most likely the softball team sat together, as teams tended to do, but Jenny had no intention of joining *that* group.

Instead, Jenny went with option D.

Be the loser who sits by herself.

She strode across the grass, keeping her distance from all the other students, and plopped down by a tree still recovering its leaves from winter. She wasn't alone in deciding to sit by herself.

Dan was there, not far away, rolled up to a deserted table. Where everywhere else people were crammed together, no one approached Dan and his table. It was like there was this ten foot forcefield around him.

He lifted his head and glared at her.

She didn't blame anyone for keeping their distance.

Jenny shoved Dan out of her thoughts and opened her boring brown lunch bag and pulled out a very normal, very boring peanut butter and jelly sandwich.

Jenny peeked between the two wheat slices. Okay. Maybe it wasn't totally boring because the jelly was actually raspberry jam—her favorite. But the second she went to take a bite, two tennis shoes came into her view. Shoes that led to a pair of jeaned legs to....

Jenny lowered her sandwich. "You've got to be kidding me."

"I knew you'd be pleased to see me." Jason dropped his backpack on the grass, which nearly landed on her leg. "Are you always this cheery?"

"Yes. Especially when people can't take the hint to leave me alone." She shoved his bag away from her. "And why aren't you with your baseball friends? Shouldn't you do the team thing or whatever it is you guys do?"

"You want me to leave you alone?" Jason asked, pretending innocence. He thumped down beside her. "I'm hurt."

Dan, she noticed, snatched up his backpack and lunch, and wheeled off. Jason noticed this too, but other than the tightening of his lips he didn't seem bothered. Dan's now empty table was immediately converged on—by the popular crowd who kept glancing in her direction.

Great.

"If I ask nicely will you go away?" she asked.

"Probably not."

Jason grinned and then dug into his own backpack and pulled out the very same brown bag as hers and tore into his sandwich, a sandwich that also looked suspiciously like hers. "But then, that's really your fault anyway."

"My fault?"

Was that a red jelly and not the usual purple?

"How is this my fault?" she asked.

"You're the one who stood up to my sister. A guy can't help but notice someone that incredibly brave… or incredibly stupid."

"I'll save you the wondering. Incredibly stupid. Now, can you go?" Because right now it felt like someone was trying to light the back of her neck on fire.

Jenny glanced over Jason's shoulders and spotted the popular crowd (anyone could spot those luscious blonde locks and designer clothes). Sure enough, she was getting the death glare by at least half the girls.

Oh.

And maybe some of the guys too.

Jason followed her gaze and Jenny snapped her attention back to her now sagging sandwich.

That's right. Jason was single. That meant no girlfriend and therefore 'claimed' by every girl who thought he was cute.

Jenny groaned. "You are nothing but trouble."

"Oh, don't worry about them."

"You're not the one they're going to try and kill with hairspray and lipstick."

She wasn't only counting the girls in that assessment. Guys could be just as vicious in defending their territory.

"You stood up to my sister," he pointed out.

"Trust me. They're scarier."

She bit into her sandwich and chewed. She'd have to steer clear of any bathrooms for the rest of the day, just in case there was a trap lying in wait. There was also the safety of her locker, which needed to be considered. Since she hadn't actually located her locker she wasn't betting on how safe it was.

Those girls would probably sneak into Mrs. Crowley's office during lunch and steal Jenny's file just to find out.

And yes, that had happened on too many occasions for her to forget the first rule of battle when it came to ridiculously hot, older students taking an interest in the new girl.

Never let your guard down.

Which was what she was trying to do.

Right now. With Jason.

Her face heated. She swallowed the lump of sandwich that suddenly didn't taste like food.

Ignoring Jason wasn't working. Not when he was sitting beside her, his leg brushing hers, acting as if he hadn't a care in the world. Or if there wasn't any other girl in the world he'd rather be sitting with.

The thought made her head spin. He shouldn't *want* to be with her. Didn't he get it? She was going to shove his sister out of the number one pitching spot and he was flirting with her!

"Is there a reason you're here?" Jenny asked, unable to hide her frustration. "I mean, right now, bothering me?"

Jason, who was finishing his sandwich (holy shit could he eat fast!), reached into his bag and pulled out a folded piece of paper.

Jenny froze. He was seriously not giving her his number.

This had to stop.

Now.

She slapped her sandwich onto her bag. "Look. You need to stop. I don't know where you get the idea that I'm interested in you, but I'm not. I don't want to eat lunch with you. I don't want to talk with you or go to the movies or whatever."

Jason lifted an eyebrow. "You're pretty intense, you know that?"

"I also don't want the entire school thinking there's something going on with us!"

She glanced over her shoulder. Damn it! There were at least six students edging closer. One had their phone out and it was pointed directly at her.

"*Is* there something between us?" Jason asked. "I wouldn't be opposed if there is."

"There isn't!"

"Really? You sure?"

She was about to start kicking him when Jason tossed the paper onto her lap. It floated there, like it hadn't a care in the world. Like it didn't understand such an innocent action was now pitting her against the entire school.

At least the female half of the population.

"Relax, okay. It's just the flier for the softball schedule. It's also got Coach Steele's number. I thought you'd be interested."

Softball schedule?

"Oh." She closed her eyes. Really? Was that the best she could do? 'Oh?' "I mean… thanks."

Because she honestly hadn't actually *wanted* his phone number. She was trying to ditch him, after all.

"You gonna give the Coach a call? Ask about trying out?"

"No."

She unfolded the paper, feeling both Jason's attention and the nearing students. Like he said, it was just a schedule with the Coach's number. It didn't have any secret coded message, no declaration of love.

"So I went to all that trouble of sneaking away Lacey's schedule and making a photocopy and you're not even going to call?" There was teasing in his voice, but something else, something sharper and deeper.

"There's no point." She tucked it into her back pocket and ignored the way her stomach plummeted to her feet. She was not disappointed. "I'm sure Chuck already did."

"Right. Your family friend."

But there was a question in that statement, almost like an expectation for her to tell him the truth. Which was just ridiculous because she didn't owe *him* anything.

"He's my trainer, okay? Dad pays him and he teaches me."

"I get it. I'm cool with it if you are."

"Yes. Now just drop it, okay?"

Jason still watched her with that grin and looking expectant. "So. About this thing between us…."

"I told you. There's nothing."

Because, there wasn't and nor would she let there be something.

"And thank you," she said. "I mean for the schedule. Chuck will appreciate it."

"I didn't do it for Chuck."

Again, there was that expectation. It hung in the air between them, charging, growing with every second until Jenny couldn't find her breath around it.

"Look. I mean it. Thank you. But I just want to be clear. I'm not looking for a boyfriend, not looking for a date for whatever dance those girls behind us are talking about. I'm probably not going to finish the season, so if that's why you came over then you can forget it."

Maybe she got a little carried away with the boyfriend comment, but her life felt like it was slipping away from her, like she was on some mountain slide and there was nothing she could do.

Nothing to hold onto.

She was falling.

Except there was Jason and for whatever reason, he kept acting like he wanted to catch her. Like he wanted to help her stop falling. Either that or he couldn't take a hint.

Jenny got up and threw her sandwich in the nearby trashcan. She wasn't hungry anyway.

"I see." Jason got up too and tossed his own bag away. "So they were right about you."

"They?"

"Yeah. In the article. Intense, focused. No social life."

"Article? What are you talking about?" Was it about her father? Another feature in the tabloids?

He stepped closer. "Hell, I'll bet you're not even going to attend the dance."

It took all of Jenny's self-control not to back up. She wouldn't show him how much he was getting to her. Or how hard it was getting to think.

"Why would I? Attend the dance, I mean."

That *wasn't* what she'd meant to ask. She'd wanted to ask about the article but her head spun from how close he was. So close she could smell the drifting of pine and summer rain off him.

"Girls do that sort of thing."

"I'm not most girls."

She was the girl with the crazy rich father, the father who came home with lipstick on his collar, who bought his daughter a personal softball trainer.

She was most definitely not most girls.

"Like I said." Jason inched closed. "Intense."

Jenny could barely breathe, could barely think. Jason was standing so close, like he didn't care who saw them, didn't care how many pictures were taken, or what anyone thought.

This was crazy. What was he doing here with her?

"And I'm glad." His breath swirled in the air, tickling her cheek.

Glad? Now she was lost. "What are you talking about?"

Her backpack slid a few inches down her shoulder and Jason settled it into place. His touch sizzled down her arm, danced like lightning off her skin, unrelenting, unforgiving.

It was like the spark simply had to show her how much he affected her. How much she didn't want him to step away. How much she didn't want his touch to go away.

Jenny stepped back and shook her head. It helped. A little.

"I'm glad," he said, "because if you hadn't so clearly stated there was nothing going on between us then there's no awkward feelings or weirdness about me saying yes."

"Yes?" She blinked. "What are you talking? I didn't ask you anything."

"Sure you did."

Jason didn't touch her. He didn't need too. She still felt the lightning as if her skin still remembered his touch.

And it did.

"You asked me to the school dance coming up. And I'm pretty sure I said yes."

TWELVE

J enny survived her first day of school. Barely. No thanks to Jason.
Jason, who even now waited beside her. This, of course, drew even more curious glances from the other waiting students. Jenny wanted the cement to open up into a sink hole and swallow her.

"I'm really sorry about those girls," Jason said for the fourth time. He tried not to glance at her cheek, but he couldn't seem to help it.

Jenny stood there, fists clenched, and used all her willpower not to smack Jason. Or continue to rub at the line of waterproof lipstick smeared on her cheek.

"If you were truly sorry, you would leave. Right now."

"This is my fault. I can't let you stand here by yourself."

"Yes. You can."

And he should because her temper really was fraying and she didn't know how much longer she'd be able to control her urge to hit him.

This was all his stupid fault. If he hadn't shown an interest in her, if he hadn't *flirted* with her, asked her to the damn dance no less, she wouldn't be standing there, after her first day of school, having barely survived an attack of the most brutal caliber.

At least she hadn't been called into the Principal's office.

Yet.

Jason shifted from one foot to the other and scratched the back of his head, but instead of making his hair look worse it just made him look perfectly rumpled and thoroughly kissed.

Ugh. This sooo wasn't fair. Not when she was the one who looked like hell and had half the school trying to kill her.

"I am sorry," he insisted. "I didn't realize Tiffany was listening."

Jenny shot a glare at him. "And what had you expected, huh? That you can just sit down, talk with me, and not expect some kind of retaliation?"

"Well, I was the one who —"

"You just don't get it. *I'm* the one they're pissed at. I'm the one they'll continue to be pissed at. And I'm the one, even now, everyone's talking about because they think *I* asked Jason Richards to the stupid dance. Which I didn't!"

She shoved him in the chest—a hard, muscular chest which only moved about an inch. No wonder he'd been able to hold off Lacey's punch.

"You sure?" Jason rubbed at his chest—in the exact spot she'd touched him. "Because you seem pretty insistent on this dance thing."

She would have killed him if she hadn't heard Chuck's rumbling, held-together-by-duct-tape truck. She'd expected her mom to pick her up, but right now she didn't care. She booked it.

Chuck's truck meant safety. It also meant no more school and no more Jason.

At least until tomorrow.

The great thing about Chuck was he didn't ask how her day went. He didn't ask about the lipstick on her cheek, didn't ask about Jason standing there looking like a dork (a very cute, attractive dork) as he waved her goodbye.

This, this was why Chuck was cool.

"Another good day, huh?"

Okay. He was cool until he *asked* about her day.

"Gee, let's see. I've now met both senior pitchers whose starting positions I'm clearly threatening. One wants to beat me up and the other wants to be my best friend. Jason won't leave me alone and got the whole female population to hate me. There was an attack while I left a bathroom which I barely survived." She indicated her cheek. "Oh! And I've apparently asked Jason to a dance, which I had no intention of doing and no intention of going to. There. Does that sound like a good day to you?"

Chuck smiled. "Sounds like you're making friends."

"I don't want friends." She shoved her backpack into the back seat. "I want everyone to leave me alone."

"Life don't work that way, darlin."

"No, especially when you're the daughter of a big famous baseball player, who by the grace of the High School gods, no one knows about yet."

Except Elizabeth. And Jason.

"Can we just go now, please?" Jenny asked.

"I can do that. But first, to add to your already good day, here." He handed her a newspaper. "I asked your mom if I could pick you up. This might not be the best time, but I figure you should hear the news from me first."

Chuck got the truck into motion, after a few sputs and starts, while Jenny flipped open the local newspaper, *The Sunny View Gazette*. On the front was a picture of her dad in his new Chargers uniform at Anaheim stadium. The article itself wasn't unusual as her dad had made the rounds of all the local papers.

"Keep reading."

She did and immediately saw the smaller, though no less eye-catching photo below it. And the title.

LOCAL CELEBRITY BRINGS CELEBRITY DAUGHTER TO THE SOFTBALL FIELD by Samantha Dawson.

"Oh no."

The photo was of Jenny standing next to her dad, a trophy nearly as tall as her in one hand, her softball glove in the other. She was smiling. Kind of. If you counted a grimace as a smile.

It was from when Jenny won the Most Valuable Player award as a freshman last year for Mountain Lake High. *This* was the article Jason had been talking about.

Jenny scanned the article, completely forgetting about her usual car sickness problems. She wanted to scream. And kill her dad.

"He didn't!" Jenny flipped to the second page where the article continued.

"He did," Chuck whispered.

Her dad had met with the local newspaper, and did an interview with them, but it wasn't an interview about him. It was about Jenny. Jenny and her prospects for playing professional softball.

"*A game changer?*" Jenny quoted. "*That with my Taylor name Jenny has the opportunity to bring in the kind of outside sponsors that will propel women's professional softball to the next level?*"

"He's not saying anything we don't already know. No harm done." Chuck reached for the newspaper, keeping his eye on the road, but Jenny snatched it away.

"No harm? This is my life! You knew about this, didn't you? You *knew* he was going to do this."

"I had a hunch." Chuck's gaze flicked to her. "When he showed you the bat. There was no other way he could have gotten his hands on one without talking you up. Only top athletes are using prototypes, testing them if you will."

"Top athletes?"

"The big name girls in the pros right now. They don't have the kind of sponsorship your dad's talking about, but he's not wrong, Jen. With your talent, with his connections… it could happen."

She wanted to throw up. Right here, right now.

"He can't…." Jenny's voice shook. "He can't do this."

Chuck didn't say anything.

This article, and everything in it, was laying the foundation for that future her dad wanted to build for Jenny. A future in professional softball.

Of course, the truth was buried under the words, within the praise he gave his daughter. After all, she was still only sixteen—but if you read between the lines, other than the giant statement about Jenny's name bringing in big sponsors, her dad's plan was laid out before her.

He really was planting those seeds, planting the idea that

someone with a famous baseball dad could maybe make softball famous, could fast-forward the whole professional women's softball league.

"The article doesn't mean nothing." Chuck ripped the newspaper from her. Not like it was hard with her hands suddenly gone numb.

Jenny's eyes filled with tears. "Nothing? It sounds like he's got everything figured out, doesn't it? Next you know, he'll be calling the top universities to see if they're interested in a pitcher-second base player."

Chuck's lips pressed into a thin line and his grip on the wheel tightened. "He's already done it."

"I… I see." Her throat went numb like her hands. "I'm not surprised."

"It doesn't mean anything," Chuck snapped. "Not unless it's what you want. No one can make you play, Jenny."

She snorted. "Oh, yes he can and you know it!"

For emphasis, she grabbed the schedule from her back pocket and threw it on the truck's dashboard.

Chuck stopped in front of light. He unfolded it.

"But I bet you don't need the schedule because you already have it, don't you?"

He folded the flier and tossed it out the window. "I do."

"Then so does my dad because you told him right?"

"Jenny."

The light changed to green. Chuck didn't move the car.

Behind them someone honked. Chuck still didn't move. He held Jenny's gaze, not moving an inch. "It's my job, Jenny. It's what he pays me for."

"Yeah. I know. I'm nothing but your job."

She crossed her arms. She refused to think why this felt like a betrayal, why it hurt so much. She'd thought Chuck might be her friend, but she was wrong. Chuck worked for her dad, end of story.

And Chuck had known, had even guessed at what her dad had planned. He'd said nothing to her. He hadn't tried to warn her.

"You don't have to play, Jenny."

The honking car gave up and zipped around them, flipping them off as he drove by.

"There's nothing I can do." She glared at him. "If Dad wants me to try out, I'll try out. And if I don't he'll just call up the coach and tell her to put me on that stupid team anyway—a team I don't even want to be on!"

Chuck looked away and finally lifted his foot off the brake. They crept forward and it felt like a lifetime before they got to the house.

Not *home*.

Jenny didn't have a home. This was just another stupid mansion she lived in. There was nothing 'home' about it.

She crossed her legs and felt something press into the pocket of her jeans. She found the taffy Elizabeth had given her, now slightly squished. She didn't need Elizabeth or Jason. Didn't need Chuck pretending to be her friend when he was just 'doing his job.'

She rolled down the manual window and chucked the taffy into her mom's stupid flowerbed. She was alone and that was just fine by her.

Friends did nothing but let you down.

THIRTEEN

J enny stared down at the recently dragged Sunny View softball field with its thin marks cutting through the infield dirt. Ready to go, ready to play.

This was the last place she wanted to be, but no amount of pleading with her parents had changed their minds. It had been a short argument. If she could even call it that.

She would try out. She would play. End of story.

From the hill's slight rise she could see the whole field below, the bleachers, the student parking in the distance now completely devoid of cars as the bell had rung fifteen minutes ago. She could even see the small shapes from the baseball players as they headed out onto the adjoining field.

Her field was still empty.

And unlike the *Angels'* practice on Sunday, these bleachers were empty except for one person, one person Jenny knew with a single glance.

Chuck.

Her hands tightened on her bat bag. She'd told him not to come. She'd known he would anyway.

"Just part of his stupid job."

Jenny's legs wobbled as the article came to her mind, as she remembered her father's words from last night, again telling her how this was for her future.

There had to be a way out. There had to be something she could do!

Lacey clamped onto Jenny's shoulder and spun her around. "Lookie here. Transfer decided to show up."

Behind Lacey was the softball team, their faces tight and ugly. There wasn't one sympathetic gaze. One girl (besides Lacey) looked like she wanted to see Jenny hung by her toes—a girl she recognized from homeroom. There was no mistaking that pinched face, that blonde ponytail high on her head like she was in the 1980s.

Jenny had already done it. She'd already stolen their smiles, their fun.

All thanks to Dad and his article.

Lacey's grip on her shirt tightened as she shifted Jenny so she could get a better look. "I see you've noticed the team. Looks like nearly everyone's accounted for."

Except Elizabeth.

Jenny didn't want to think about her sudden relief, the exhale of breath as she realized this. But it didn't matter. Elizabeth was probably running late.

"I'm bettin' you're also a smart girl," Lacey tapped Jenny's forehead, "and noticed no one seems too happy you're here. Do you need another good long look, huh, Transfer? Enough to realize you ain't wanted here and should pack up your bat and never set foot on our field again?"

Jenny couldn't control which school she went to, which team she played for, but she could control this.

She could stand up to Lacey.

And just like that, Jenny had an idea. The second she got into a fight with the Sunny View star pitcher, she'd be off the team. Not even her dad could do anything about it.

Ignoring Lacey's grip wasn't easy, but Jenny cocked a hip and placed a hand on top. The thing with bullies was you needed to understand how they worked, how to set them up and play them—just like she did with any batter.

She'd throw a fastball, tight and inside, to back Lacey off.

"You know, Lacey. This is actually a first for me."

"First? What the hell are you talking about?"

"I haven't even set foot on the field and you've already got the whole team ready to beat the shit out of me. Even the lowly bench warmer freshmen."

The girls grumbled. Some tossed balls into their mitts. Loud, leather-smacking sounds filled the air.

No way would this 'family' stand for Jenny's attitude. She could see it in their eyes.

Jenny smiled.

This, of course, only pissed Lacey off more. The girl's face scrunched tight making her look more like a boy. Her other hand darted out and grabbed another fistful of Jenny's shirt.

"Who the hell do you think you are, Transfer? You think you're some softball goddess who can just swoop in and hand us the Division Championship?"

"Last I checked I hadn't called myself a goddess of anything. And last I checked, it's not my fault you haven't won the Championship. How many chances have you had now, Lacey, three years?"

The girl with the '80s ponytail stepped forward. "The hell with her, Lacey! We don't need her rich arm on this team. We'll win the Division without her."

Lacey shook Jenny. Hard. "Alice's right. We don't care how rich and famous your daddy is. We don't need no transfer player like you on our team and we sure as hell don't *want* you on our team."

"Oh. So you'd figured it out, huh?" Jenny said in between shakes. "Realized who my dad was and all his big pro plans for me?"

Lacey's face blistered to a dark red color.

Just a bit more. A little more push and Lacey would pummel her.

It was a good plan.

At least, until *he* showed up.

"Lace! That's enough." Jason pushed his way through the girls and practically barreled Alice over as she tried to get in his way.

Jason's relaxed, easy-going attitude was gone. He was a completely different person. Intense, focused, and pissed off as all hell.

Lacey's grip slackened. "Jason."

There was shock in her voice.

Alice grabbed for Jason's arm. "Stay out of this, Jason. It's none of your business."

He slid out from her grasp. "Shove it, Alice."

Then, all his attention was on Lacey. "You gonna tell me this isn't what it looks like?"

He didn't wait for her answer. He pulled Jenny away from Lacey, hands soft but firm, and placed her behind him. Jenny's vision went a little dizzy, both from the caring way he touched her, and the spark she felt reignite. It was like his touch alone was enough for her to remember… to want….

He couldn't care about her. This was wrong. He was supposed to be siding with his sister—not her! "Jason. I'm fine. I don't need —"

"My protection. Of course not. You were just going to let her beat the crap out of you." He shot a narrowed look over his shoulder—a look that shut Jenny's mouth fast. "Something no sane person would do. We'll talk later."

Somehow he knew there was more to it, that there was a reason why she wanted to fight Lacey.

"This isn't your business," Lacey growled.

Jason's attention whirled back to Lacey and he matched her, stance for stance, legs spread, hands on hips. "And what's mom going to say, huh? What's she going to say when she finds out you're still bullying the new kids?"

"Mom's not around." Spit poured from Lacey's lips. "And even if she was, whatever the hell I do ain't her business. Just like this isn't yours. Butt out."

"The hell I will." It was like every second he was growing taller, as if his force of will alone could tower over Lacey.

The other girls were confused, unsure of what to do. They'd been prepared to deal with Jenny. They hadn't been prepared for a fight between siblings.

Two very scary siblings.

"You may not like Jenny," Jason to them, "you may hate her, but if you want any chance of beating Mount Crest this year you're going to need her. And I'd say giving Jenny the cold shoulder on her first day is a pretty damn stupid mistake."

"She's not a member of this team and neither are you," Lacey snapped. "Just because you stopped playing and parked your ass in our bleachers doesn't make this any of your business."

Jenny felt the way his body tensed, felt the tightly coiled anger simmering off his skin. She couldn't see his face. She wanted too. She didn't know why.

But Jason wasn't her problem. The team was. Her father and his plans were.

She had to do something. Now. Before it was too late.

Jenny slid out from behind him and faced Lacey and the rest of the girls. "I don't need you to defend me, Jason. If they don't want me on their team, fine. I'll find someone who does. Maybe someone like Mount Crest."

If only Coach Steele and Elizabeth hadn't also shown up. Maybe if they hadn't she'd have still gotten her fight—and a sure fire way off the team.

If only life were that simple.

FOURTEEN

"What the hell is going on?" The softball coach's voice boomed across the field.

The girls stumbled back, dropped their bats and let softballs roll to the ground. But it was too late. Their coach had seen everything—and had ruined Jenny's chances.

The coach stomped towards the team, long legs in white shorts easily covering the distance, her muscular arms swinging at her side. Even from here Jenny could make out the fury in her gaze as she glared at her team.

Elizabeth and another woman jogged alongside the coach, both determined, both pissed. Jenny recognized the woman from the *Angels* practice on Sunday. Coach Laurie. Elizabeth's stepmother.

Seeing Elizabeth, blonde hair tied back in twin braids, wearing the team's blue practice shirt, made Jenny pause, hesitate. Elizabeth hadn't sided with the team. She'd gotten the coach instead.

Elizabeth didn't fool around.

Lacey backed away from Jenny, but it was too late for her.

"Lacey. You're benched for the next two games."

Horror swept through the team.

"Coach!"

"You can't!"

The voices rose up in protest, then died as their coach swung her attention to the girls. They wilted and shut up.

"That goes for all of you. I see you acting up in any way, against Jenny, against any new girl, you're out. Do I make myself clear?"

Heads nodded.

"Good. Now get warming." Lacey moved to follow, but the coach shook her head. "Not you Lacey. Laurie, you'll take care of this?"

"Already done." Laurie, who looked just as athletic and capable as the other coach, gestured for Lacey to follow her. "Let's go to the bleachers, Lacey."

Lacey didn't go quietly. She grabbed her bag and threw it on the metal benches. The crashing sound echoed across the field.

The coach ignored Lacey's display of temper, letting Laurie handle it. She, however, didn't ignore Jenny. "I'm sorry. I expected more from her—from the whole team. There's no excuse for how they treated you. I'm Coach Steele."

She held out her hand.

Jenny reluctantly shook the coach's hand and glanced at the bleachers where Chuck sat not far from Lacey. Like Laurie, he was also acting like her temper didn't bother him.

She knew better. He'd be watching Lacey, watching to see if she really was a threat to his 'charge.'

Jenny dropped Steele's hand. "It's fine. I'm used to it."

"Not on my team. Not ever again."

Coach Steele glanced at both Jason and Elizabeth who were still waiting protectively at Jenny's back. "Don't know how you did it, but you've already got yourself some back-up. I'm glad."

Jenny wasn't, not really, not when there went her one shot off this team. She didn't say anything.

"I talked with your Chuck last week. He said you're a hell of a player."

Jenny shrugged. This was no news to her.

Steele smirked. "Of course, that don't mean much when you've already formed an opinion of your own."

"Already?"

"That's right," Steele said. "I saw you play at the Tri-Ace Tournament, but why don't we see what you can do here, huh? Grab your gear. Elizabeth, you'll warm her up?"

"Sure thing, Coach." Elizabeth slipped her hand in Jenny's arm. "Come on. I can't pitch yet, but I've been cleared to throw the ball some."

"If," Steele interjected, "you take it easy."

Jenny didn't have a chance to grab her bag from the ground—Jason got it instead. He held the bag for her, but when she slipped the strap under her shoulder, he stepped back, head turned away from her.

He wouldn't meet her eyes, even when she mumbled "thanks."

She didn't know why this bothered her, but with the team still glaring at her from their stretching spot in the outfield, she let the matter of Jason drop. She had bigger problems to deal with.

Like surviving practice.

Practice. As if she could call 'this' practice. It was more like an Olympic try-out through the fiery hells of scorching softballs. Jenny could hit. Jenny could throw, field, and pitch just fine. Even when she wasn't 'trying' she still did just fine.

It wasn't the softball part that made this the worst try-out of her life. It was how very much the girls hated her—and how they actively tried to bring her down.

With Lacey busted to the benches, apparently it was up to Alice to pick up the slack, and when she threw the *sixth* rise ball tight and inside at Jenny's chin, it wasn't difficult to figure out who was keeping the fight still flaming.

"Alice," Steele warned from the third base.

"Sorry, Coach. It slipped." Alice tossed her ponytail over her shoulder and grinned at Jenny, all teeth and no trace of an apology.

Jenny dug her cleat into the ground and gave her bat (hers, not the fancy one her dad got her), another warm up swing. Fine. If Alice didn't want to play nice, then Jenny didn't have to either.

The next pitch was in the same spot, but Jenny was ready for it. She got her bat out fast, hitting the ball before it could jam her swing.

Instead of being an 'easy out' Jenny smacked the crap out of the ball, easily pulling it into left field. Coach Steele clapped.

Jenny lowered her bat and shrugged at Alice, who fumed on the mound. "Want to throw another one at my head? Be my guest."

And that was pretty much how practice went. She *should* have played terrible, her next best chance of not making the team, but with Chuck watching he'd know if she tried to tank her try-out. The best Jenny could hope for was another confrontation, and with Lacey out of the game, that meant pushing Alice.

But no matter how much she baited Alice right back, her fellow homeroom classmate refused to step over that line. So instead of Jenny getting into a fight or being asked to leave, she got a big ass handshake from Coach Steele the second practice ended.

"You've got a place on this team if you're still up for it, and I hope you still are."

What else could Jenny say to that? No?

Like that would work. Her dad wouldn't let her.

She managed a wobbly smile. "Great. Thanks."

"Better yet," Steele said, "we're playing Skyline on Thursday and I want you to start."

From the corner of her eye, Jenny saw Alice tense in the dugout and throw her glove at the fence.

"Are you, uh, sure about that? I mean, I don't want to —"

"Lacey's benched and Elizabeth isn't up to pitching yet." Steele dropped Jenny's hand. "Skyline's a tough team, right up there with Mount Crest. I need experience on the mound and frankly, I'd like to see what you can do."

Steele leaned in so only Jenny could hear. "I also want to see what you can do with the pressure… and with this team behind you."

It felt like Jenny's whole world flaked away, piece by piece. After one practice Steele already believed in her softball ability—and her ability to play nice. Hadn't the coach *heard* her and Alice going at it?

But Steele didn't wait for Jenny's answer. Instead, she clapped Jenny on the back and told the team to pack it in.

Some parents had arrived, those needing to give rides to their kids, and Jenny spotted Chuck's retreating form, alone and silent as he went back to his truck to wait for her. Normally he was in the thick of things with the parents, shaking hands and chatting away. Not this time.

Not like she cared either.

After all, he'd gotten what he wanted.

Jenny had made the team.

FIFTEEN

School was going about as well as it always did, which for Jenny meant 'not good.'

For anyone standing on the outside looking in, they'd think 'great.'

Great was sooo not what she was experiencing.

The girl whose name Jenny had already forgotten with her luscious blonde hair, manicured nails, and pink leather Coach purse, waved at the classroom. "Here you are! Biology, as promised. Now wasn't that better than spending ten minutes searching by yourself?"

No.

Jenny grimaced. "Thanks."

It took a little maneuvering, but she managed to get the Barbie look-alike off her. Just another day at a school who suddenly found out just 'who' the new girl was. She'd gotten good over the years at ditching the leeches, but some managed to hold on for an extra day or two. Like Barbie.

Jenny recognized the two-person lab tables, always black so you couldn't 'see' what was spilled (and what had never been successfully cleaned up). The only problem with this set up was the class was already filled, leaving only one empty chair.

A chair that just happened to be next to Alice.

Now, while Jenny was all for getting Alice mad on the field (and hopefully getting Jenny off the team), fighting at school would not be good. That's the kind of thing that stayed on your permanent record and while Jenny didn't give a rat's ass about softball, she *did* care about school.

As if sensing Jenny's presence (or noticing the sudden quiet), Alice glanced up from the paper she was doodling on. Her dark gaze honed in on Jenny and she snarled.

Okay. So maybe Alice didn't care so much about school as she did softball. This should be a fun class.

Still, the sound Alice made was impressive, at least until the teacher—Professor Bingley—thanked Alice for volunteering to be Jenny's partner. The next thing Jenny knew the squat, balding man in the buttoned-up white lab coat had ushered her towards the back of the class and into the table with Alice.

No escape. She simply had to suck it up and deal with her.

Alice, however, didn't move her backpack from Jenny's spot. "First you steal my spot on the team and now I have to share a table with you?"

"First off, I didn't steal anything. You want to beat me out, fine. Pitch better than me." Jenny shoved Alice's backpack over. "And I'm all for not sitting next to you. I'm sure there's plenty of people who'd love to switch with you."

Alice bit her bottom lip, as if the pain was the only thing keeping back her temper.

Jenny might have said something, might have indeed switched with one of the guys in front of their table who were clearly interested in doing just that, but Professor Bingley called class to order. It looked like she and Alice were stuck.

As lab partners.

Great.

Jenny pulled out her *Intro to Biology* textbook, half-wished her parents had picked a school more up to speed on the e-texts like she'd had in San Diego, and then did her best to ignore Alice.

Tried to, anyway as Alice was making ignoring her very, very difficult. Like every other minute she'd knock off Jenny's pencil, step on her shoe, or 'accidentally' nudge her.

Jenny grit her teeth. She'd been so focused on getting Lacey and Elizabeth upset, she'd completely forgotten about the younger, more vulnerable players. Players like Alice. Girls who played fine but were still developing… until Jenny neatly came in and slid Alice further back into the rotation.

Okay. Jenny could see why Alice didn't like her, resented her even, but spiteful?

They were in middle of dissecting a frog, something Jenny had done a half dozen times already, when Alice 'accidentally' flicked frog guts all over Jenny's white shirt.

"Oops." Alice smiled sweetly.

Jenny glanced down at the putrid brown color now staining her new shirt. "Thanks."

"Well, you are *supposed* to wear old clothes over your school ones, but then I doubt you even *have* any old clothes."

The two guys in front of them snickered, then glanced away when Jenny glared at them. Professor Bingley, with his unfortunate good timing, interrupted Jenny before she could bite out another reply to Alice and instructed her to go wash off.

Fine with her. She didn't want to be in this stupid class with Alice as her stupid partner anyway.

Jenny snagged her backpack and stomped out. What was she going to do? Frog guts didn't exactly come clean off shirts—and she had the rest of the day to survive.

She passed by an open door in the biology hallway and stopped when someone called her name. Laurie stood in the doorway, no longer wearing her softball shorts and cleats, but neatly pressed black pants and a button up midnight blouse.

Great. Just freakin' great. She'd forgotten Laurie was a teacher here too.

"I thought that was you." Laurie's attention flicked to Jenny's frog stained shirt. "More trouble, huh? Alice?"

"How did you…?"

"They're my girls. I know them. Come on. I've got something that'll take that right out." She moved towards the back of the classroom with its same black tables, and pulled down a detergent box from a cabinet. "I've got something else you can wear until it dries. Come on, then. You've changed in front of enough girls I'm sure you won't mind me."

That wasn't what Jenny minded. It was Laurie's niceness, her kindness—neither of which she deserved.

After all, wasn't it Jenny who'd taken away the smiles of Laurie's girls?

"I don't, I mean, I can't."

Laurie paused over the sink. "You're not talking about being shy, are you?"

"Why are you being so nice to me? I've ruined everything for your team. They're mad, they're not having fun." More than a few wanted to kill her. "You should hate me."

Laurie turned off the faucet. "I'm being nice because you deserve it. You haven't done anything and you haven't ruined this team either. They're nervous, they're scared. They see you as a threat, but I don't think you are. Elizabeth doesn't think you are either."

Laurie held out her hand, waiting for Jenny's shirt. Jenny didn't move, didn't know if she could.

"But what if I am? What if I am a threat?" Because she was.

"Then they'll grow. They'll become a stronger team or they won't. But that's on them and not you." Laurie still waited for the frog-stained shirt. "I think you'll be good for them and they'll be good for you."

Jenny didn't believe her. Not after biology class with Alice.

Still, she was stuck until she found a way off this team and into another school.

She didn't know why she'd said anything to Laurie. Maybe because she'd been like Jenny once, had known how tough the game was, how hard you worked if you wanted to succeed.

Jenny closed the classroom door and pulled off her shirt. "You quit, didn't you? Softball, I mean."

"I did."

Quit. The word was so foreign to Jenny, like it didn't belong in the same sentence as softball.

"How?"

The word tumbled out of Jenny's mouth. She didn't know why, didn't know where it came from, but there it was. She couldn't take it back.

Laurie tilted her head to the side, bangs brushing against her eyebrows. "It wasn't easy, probably one of the hardest things I've ever done—at least, until I started the *Angels* and met Elizabeth's dad, but that's another story and a different kind of hard. But back then, when I was only a couple years older than you, I needed to walk away. I needed to leave the game and I'm glad I did."

"But… but what about your parents?"

Again, Jenny had lost control over her mouth but the truth was she wanted to know, wanted to hear from someone else who'd been down this similar, though not the same road, as Jenny.

"It devastated my father. For years. Then, we found our way around it. I know this isn't easy, Jenny. I know how hard you're working—I also know what kind of future your dad wants for you."

How? Jenny backed up, not realizing she'd moved until her butt hit a table. How could she know?

"But," Laurie said, with a small smile, "your future is yours. Even if he doesn't like it. And you know the best thing?"

"What?"

"The best thing is at the end of the day, you won't be standing alone." Laurie handed Jenny a Tigers softball practice shirt to wear while hers soaked. "You'll have a whole family behind you."

SIXTEEN

N ice shirt."

Jenny fumbled with her sandwich as Jason's worn, previously white-colored sneakers popped into view. What was *he* doing here?

"Getting on your softball team spirit, huh?"

"I, uh, had an accident in biology. Laurie lent it to me."

"Laurie."

Jason clutched his brown lunch bag in one hand, lips pressed into a thin line. After a slight hesitation, he sank down on the grass beside her. Unlike yesterday's lunch when he was relaxed and teasing, hell even flirting with her, now he was tense. Back straight, shoulders tall.

Not a hint of flirting in him.

Part of her almost liked the flirting better.

A small, small part of her.

"You, uh, gonna eat with me again?" she asked.

"You don't want me to?"

"No." Yes. "I mean, I thought you were mad at me. Because of yesterday."

He snorted. "Was and still am. Which reminds me you gonna tell me what the hell that was about?"

Jenny unzipped her sandwich bag and took a bite to buy her some time. Why did Jason care? And why—if he was still mad—was he sitting with her?

She remembered her conversation with Laurie, about not being alone, about needing the team. Well, she didn't need the *team*. She was fine on her own....

But maybe she needed somebody. Somebody who'd listen. A friend, a friend like Chuck had been before he turned to the dark side.

"Okay," she said. "Fine. I was trying to do exactly what you thought."

Jason dumped the contents of his lunch onto the grass—sandwich, apple, Doritos bag. "Trying to get my sister to beat the shit out of you? Do you have a death wish or something?"

"Maybe. I just… I just didn't want to play."

"Seriously?" he asked. "You were trying *not* to make the team?"

"Maybe." But she didn't put much emphasis behind it. "I mean, it sounded like a good idea at the time. Get into a fight with the star player, lose my chance for the team. Not even my dad could argue with that."

"Your dad."

Jason didn't look at her for a moment, simply concentrated on his sandwich as if it was the greatest lunch he could possibly have, so Jenny did the same.

This was definitely getting into territory that Jenny didn't want to talk about—so why was she telling him?

"Your dad's the reason, isn't he?" Jason asked. "What he said about you in the paper, about playing pro ball? That's why you don't want to play?"

It was too close to the mark, way too close. "I don't want to play for this team," she said instead. "They're a family. I ruin families."

"I don't think that and you shouldn't either."

Yeah, well his sister and the whole stupid team did. Jenny was sure they couldn't all be wrong about her.

Jason took a slow bite of his sandwich. He glanced away. "If you… if you didn't make the team, would you have switched schools?"

"Probably."

"Then you'd miss the dance."

Jenny nearly spit out her own half-chewed sandwich. "I wasn't going with you anyway."

He didn't say anything. About the dance. Not about her dad.

"I get it." Jason wiped some crumbs from the side of his mouth. "All parents have plans for their kids, probably your dad more so than most, but I don't think getting a black eye or two is the right choice."

Jenny ignored the one crumb that clung to his lower lip. Or tried too. She caught her hand lifting to wipe it away. "Clearly not. After all, my plan didn't work."

"Probably because Lacey didn't actually hit you. Trust me. That's a good thing." He leaned back in the grass, using his arms to brace him as he stared at her.

That look in his eyes, so intense, so worried. It took her breath away, which wasn't good since she was in the midst of swallowing. She coughed to keep from choking as her food went down the wrong pipe.

"Hey, take it easy. Here." Jason pressed a water bottle into her hand. "Drink."

She did. And tried to still her thundering heart. It didn't listen. And Jason didn't leave either, not even when she handed back his bottle and said thank you.

"Opening Day is Friday, right. You going?"

Opening Day? Why would he know or care?

"You a Chargers fan?" she asked instead.

"Nope."

Great. Jenny closed her eyes, knowing she—and her dad—must be the reason Jason knew about Opening Day. "Yes. I go every year. For every team. It's no big deal."

Jason nodded. "It's a big deal for him. He'll be glad you're there."

"Whatever. I don't care."

Jason's eyebrow lifted. "I'm sensing the 'you don't care too much' attitude about your dad and baseball."

She looked away. "I don't like what it does to him."

"Yeah. I've seen the papers. I'm sorry."

And he was. She could hear it in his voice, could see it in the way he looked at her. He was sorry; sorry she had to go to such lengths as getting into a fight with Lacey to get kicked off a team.

She tried to let it go like it was no big deal, to let it roll off of her. But Jason knew. He knew it really hurt her.

Jason shifted on the grass, which meant another inch closer to her. "It's okay, you know. To be mad. To hate him. To hate the women who take advantage of him."

"Advantage? Of *him*? Are we talking about the same person here?"

Jason's eyes got a faraway look as he stared at the street opposite them. She had a feeling he saw something more than the passing cars or the wrinkled Asian woman walking her fluffy snowball of a dog.

"Jason?"

He still didn't look at her.

"I know about baseball and the big leagues," he said. "I know what it can do to people, being in the spotlight. Most players are just regular guys. They don't know how to deal with that. They don't know how to say no."

Saying no. The way he said it….

"Then again," he went on, still lost in his own thoughts, "some guys are smart and get out of the game before it gets too rough."

Get out of the game.

Like her dad hadn't done.

Jason. And she remembered seeing him in a letterman jacket, hanging with the baseball players like he was part of them—but not. Like he was separate.

"Like you, you mean?"

"I don't play baseball."

She caught the tail-end of longing in his voice, a wisp of something deeper, something he was trying to hide from her. "But you did, didn't you? You used to play baseball."

"I did. A long time ago. I don't anymore."

She wanted to ask why. Wanted to know why he'd given it up and why it so clearly pained him. The thought… the thought of giving up softball was foreign to her. Impossible.

"Anyway," he said, "all I'm saying is there's more to your dad's story—the women, the tabloids, baseball, everything—and if it bothers you this much you should ask him about it. Confront him."

She snorted. "I've tried that and I get grounded."

Not to mention confronting her dad was her mom's job. Not hers.

Still, if her mom hadn't said anything in all these years, Jenny wasn't dumb enough to believe she'd stand up for their family any time soon.

"You can always keep trying."

"No thanks," Jenny said. "I think I'll just survive another school year and then he'll just ship me off again when he's traded."

Which always happened just as they got settled in.

"That's… that's too bad."

Jason closed his eyes and she wondered what he was thinking about, wondered what had caused him to smile in just that way. A small smile, like a secret smile. "I think you'd fit in here, in Sunny View."

With you? She wanted to ask.

Which was silly, totally silly. Besides, the daughter of a famous softball dad didn't fit in *anywhere*.

"So," Jason propped himself back into a sitting position and tapped the brim of her hat, "you taking anyone with you to the game?"

"Like you?"

Okay, now *she* was flirting with him! So not cool. And so not allowed. But she couldn't help it.

Jason grinned. "You asking me? Because if you were, I might say yes."

SEVENTEEN

J enny managed to get out of lunch without asking Jason to Opening Day. Unfortunately, Elizabeth decided to pay a visit and had overheard. Now she was pushing Jenny to change her mind—even if Jenny had said no a zillion times.

In fact, Elizabeth was *still* pestering Jenny the next day. And at 8:00 in the morning when her head was stuffed with cotton candy, eyes baggy and crusty, and unable to stop yawning—the last thing Jenny wanted to talk about was boys.

Jason, in particular.

"Look." Jenny slammed her barely-holding-onto-the-wall locker shut. "I don't want to talk about this. I'm tired, I'm grumpy, I have to pitch on a team who clearly hates me, and the last thing I want to talk about is Jason!"

Elizabeth shifted the two textbooks in her arms. "Really? How else do you feel?"

Jenny huffed and stormed towards her homeroom, but Elizabeth was fast—even in those two inch heeled boots.

"Oh, come on, Jenny. It was a joke." She blocked the double doors. "You don't need to ask Jason, but I think you should."

"Well, I'm not going to." She'd either have to go the long way around or go through Elizabeth. Right now, going through Elizabeth sounded like a good idea.

She hoped Laurie would forgive her. Later.

"Okay, fine." Elizabeth spread her feet wider, grounding herself as if she knew Jenny was thinking about going through her.

Damn, pitcher.

"If you don't want to ask Jason, you should ask someone else."

"I don't know anyone and I'm not asking you, so don't ask." Jenny pushed past Elizabeth, who surprisingly, let her go.

In truth, asking Elizabeth would be the easiest solution. One, it would get her mom off her back about 'making friends' and also… well Elizabeth was the closest thing to a friend Jenny had.

But she didn't want to. Not when seeing Elizabeth there, seeing how their two lives could have been so different—if Jenny's dad had walked away from baseball instead of Elizabeth's.

She shook her head.

No. It hadn't happened that way. Wishing or even dreaming wasn't going to change anything.

The fact was it'd simply hurt too much to see Elizabeth there. So she wasn't taking anyone.

Elizabeth had somehow, even in those boots, kept pace with her. "I won't ask you again about it, okay?"

"Thank you."

She nodded, as if she'd expected nothing less. "Now, you're going to sit with us at lunch today, right?"

Jenny froze and the students behind her cursed as they almost ran into her. "Lunch?"

"It's tradition. The team eats together before a game." Elizabeth patted Jenny's arm. "Don't worry. It'll be fine. You're part of the team now."

Without waiting for Jenny's stammered, 'No way in hell,' Elizabeth ditched her, leaving Jenny standing in the middle of the hallway with its faded carpet and the throngs of students glancing at her, wondering if they should step forward and introduce themselves to the famous guy's daughter.

Up ahead, Jenny spotted Jason heading into his class, wearing the same letterman jacket as if it was like a second skin. He paused for a moment, eyes searching hers, and waited.

Waiting for her?

She had no intention of doing anything of the sort, so why her feet were suddenly carrying her down the halls just as fast as Elizabeth in her boots, Jenny had no idea.

But then Alice came from the other direction and beside her was Dan in his wheelchair, carrying around his gloomy, dark raincloud. Jenny was close enough to hear their conversation, Alice asking Dan if he was coming to the game and Dan's sharp reply.

"Will Jason be there?"

"Probably."

"Then no."

Up to this point, Jason had only eyes for Jenny, but he straightened when Dan said his name, which Dan noticed. Lightning sparked from his raincloud as he glared at Jason.

Alice's face whitened... then turned into the grimace Jenny was sooo very familiar with. Had she and Jason been a couple? Was that the look she saw pass between them? So then how did Dan fit into it?

Jenny's heart thudded, loud. This wasn't something she wanted to think about.

Not once did Jason look back at Jenny. He simply nodded at the two, mumbled a good morning, and ducked into his homeroom. He didn't wait to talk with her—as if he'd forgotten she was even there. Meanwhile Dan sped down the hall, practically running Jenny over.

"Well, I guess you showed up." Alice blocked the doorway, forcing Jenny to stop. "We had a bet going, you know?"

She shouldn't say anything. She knew she shouldn't. She couldn't help it.

"A bet, huh? Like how many girls I'm going to strike out?"

Alice tossed her long-ass ponytail over her shoulder, hiked her backpack up on her shoulder, and laughed. There was nothing nice or musical about her laugh.

It was pure, mean, bitch laugh.

"A bet if you'd even show your face after such a *wonderful* first day."

Right. As if Jenny could have expected anything less. "Well, I'm guessing you lost."

Jenny shoved Alice to the side, using her legs muscles from all that pitching to push off the ground. Alice stumbled back into the door and Jenny forced a smile down as their teacher looked her way. Nothing to see here, she thought.

Not yet anyway. Not until after the game, until she showed this stupid team just how badly they needed her.

And how badly they'd hurt when she stopped playing for them.

Because she would. She just had to find a way.

EIGHTEEN

As promised, Elizabeth found Jenny at the end another tortuous biology class with the wonderful Alice as her partner (before she managed to sneak into the library to avoid the promised team lunch).

"Thought you could get away, didn't you?" Elizabeth grinned, and then slid in front of Alice when she tried to zip by her. "I don't know where you're going, but you have a lunch date too."

Alice sneered. "I'm not eating with *her.*"

"Yes. You are."

The rest of the class had already gone, bolted as soon as the bell rang. Still, one or two lingered outside in the halls and it wouldn't take much to get their attention. Raised voices, which then led to shoving and possibly fighting, tended to draw a crowd.

Jenny didn't want a crowd.

She just wanted to be left alone.

Too bad Elizabeth wasn't about to let that happen.

"Look, just forget it." Jenny dropped her backpack onto the lab table, the loud 'boom' making Alice jump. Either that or it was Alice's realization that Elizabeth was getting in her face and going to drop-kick her in a moment.

"If she can't stomach her food around me don't force her."

"I can't," Alice snapped. "The very sight of you makes my stomach churn."

"Too bad," Elizabeth said. "We're a team. We eat together, even if we don't like each other."

"Whatever." Jenny slipped her bag on her shoulder and grabbed her almost empty water bottle. "I just need to give something to Laurie first."

Elizabeth didn't seem to mind, but Alice clearly did—especially when Jenny handed Laurie the recently washed practice shirt she'd let Jenny borrow.

Laurie's gaze flicked once to Alice. She gave Jenny back her now washed, stain-free shirt. "No stain, as promised."

Alice paled.

"Thanks." Actually, Jenny was surprised to realize she was grateful for Laurie. Not so much for cleaning her shirt but because she'd kept her promise.

No one kept their promises to her. Mostly because she was never around long enough for them to be kept.

"You remember what I told you?" Laurie asked, but this she said to Alice. Not to Jenny.

"Yeah. Sure," Alice mumbled.

"Good. I'll see you guys at the game today. Kick ass." She gave Jenny a hard squeeze, hugged Elizabeth, then shooed them out of her room.

The three girls left the building, Alice practically being dragged by Elizabeth. Elizabeth, it turned out, had a really scary glare, and even Jenny found herself keeping her head down. That girl might be sunshine, but when she was mad… there was no mistaking it. You jumped when she told you to.

"I learned it from Laurie," Elizabeth answered as if she knew what was on Jenny's mind.

"In that case, I don't want to play for her either."

Alice laughed. "As if. You'd *never* play on the *Angels* even if Coach Steele is *allowing* you to play on the school team. But you're not, and never will be, *Angels* material."

"She would." Elizabeth poked Alice. "Maybe it's you we don't need on the team anymore. You know what Laurie says about attitudes."

Alice swallowed. She didn't apologize though, which was just as well. Being on one team with Alice (not to mention the rest of the girls) was bad enough.

Two teams?

No freakin' way.

As far as Jenny was concerned, Laurie and Elizabeth could work as much magic as they liked, but nothing was going to change between Jenny and the team. For example, this was most likely going to be the worst lunch of Jenny's entire high-school career.

To think she'd been trying to ditch Jason since she'd met him.

The second she spotted the team in the far corner of the lunch table area, the one shaded by the only tree, Jenny immediately missed Jason.

She wanted his company. Now. Anything but the glares of thirteen pissed-off girls.

"Second thoughts?" Alice asked, her voice sweet.

"You wish."

It was a bravado answer, but it worked. At least, the way Alice scowled and stomped to the safety of her team said it worked. Of course, now came the harder part, the playing tough and acting tough.

Jenny squeezed her eyes closed. She could do this. They didn't want her, fine. She didn't want them. But that didn't mean she couldn't show them exactly what she was made out of first.

"You okay?" Elizabeth lingered by her side. "I know they're not acting very nice, but they're a great bunch of girls."

"So I heard."

Lacey trying to punch her and Alice's frog guts notwithstanding.

"Just do your best on the field today and they'll come around. You'll see," Elizabeth said. "Besides, we need you. Even if they're too thick-headed to realize it."

It didn't matter. All she had to do was survive lunch, right?

She could do that. Maybe.

Lacey jumped onto the top of the table, arms braced on her hips.

She had eyes only for Jenny. Beside her was Alice, who flicked the end of her ponytail back and forth.

"Did I say thick-headed?" Elizabeth murmured. "How about idiotic bitches?"

"That," Jenny said, unable to help her own answering smile, "I can agree with."

First step, survive lunch.

Second step, survive the game.

Dealing with high school by itself was bad enough. Throw in girls and softball, and the playing field just got a whole lot muddier.

NINETEEN

There was no way she'd survive lunch. Not without a miracle.

Jenny ignored the crowded bench and set her bag on the grass as far from the team as she could get and still say she was 'with' them. Elizabeth shot her an exasperated look, but she didn't say anything. All Jenny had to do was keep her head down and eat her sandwich.

How difficult could that be?

Easy. No problem.

"There you are." Jason dropped his heavy backpack and barely missed squishing her leg.

A miracle! Jenny wiped the grin off her face before Jason noticed. "I wondered if you were going to show up."

"And miss eating with you? Wouldn't miss it." He grinned back and winked.

Damn it. He knew how excited she was to see him.

"Besides," he said, "I forgot there was a game today. Got all the way to our spot before I remembered."

Our spot? Jenny stilled the flutter in her chest. "Yeah. I wasn't exactly given a choice."

From the table, Lacey snorted, clearly listening in but Jason just ignored her—her and everyone else. He only had eyes for Jenny and *that* was not helping that flutter in her chest one bit.

She tucked her legs underneath her, hoping to keep every inch of her as far from him as possible. It didn't help that by him just sitting there, bare few feet from her, set that spark in her stomach flying. It was like just seeing Jason gave it a whole new charge, a whole new zip.

For once though, Jason didn't pester her. He let her eat her sandwich in relative peace, exchanged a few words with the softball team, but for the most part he kept quiet.

Which was really, really unusual for him.

After his silence stretched to the longest five minutes she'd ever experienced, Jenny glanced at him—and realized he'd stopped eating and was staring at the baseball team across from them.

No. Staring wasn't the right word.

She didn't know if there was a right word. Longing. Like an ache she sometimes felt when she wondered what it'd be like to have a real home, a normal family.

But then he realized she was watching and the look vanished. He took a chunk out of his sandwich.

Lacey, who must have also noticed, asked him how the baseball team was doing this year.

"Good." Jason's attention was completely on his sandwich, but Jenny wasn't fooled and neither was Lacey.

This perked up Elizabeth's attention, while Alice, Jenny noticed, moved to the other end of the bench. It was like she was moving as far from Jenny as she could. How was this Jenny's fault? For once she hadn't actually *done* anything.

"How's that new freshman ace of theirs coming along?" Elizabeth asked.

"Blake? Uh, good. Really good. Just needs more experience."

"Jason's been working with him," Lacey offered.

This perked up Jenny's attention. "Really? You never mentioned that. You were a pitcher too?"

Of course, Jason never mentioned anything about baseball.

One of the baseball players, tall with a pimply face that could only belong to a freshman, was staring at the girls. Or in particular, staring at Jenny.

She blushed. No guy should have those kind of puppy dog eyes.

Jason laughed at Jenny's reaction. "Don't worry. He's not staring at you because he wants to ask you to 'that' dance. Just wants your dad's autograph. Desperately."

"Oh."

"What's that, Jason?" Lacey asked. "Dance? I thought you said the dance was stupid and you wouldn't be caught dead in a penguin suit?"

Jenny's blush deepened, which caused Jason's grin to widen.

"That's what I thought until Jenny picked a fight with you. Any girl who's tough enough to stand up to you forced me to reevaluate his options. What can I say? She swept me off my feet."

This was sooo not cool. How did this happen?

For the team, however, this seemed to be exactly what they needed. They laughed and Jenny felt the tension in the air lessening, as if the teasing banter between the two siblings—which was about her—was enough for them to relax, to come to terms that she was sitting with them, eating lunch before a game.

Elizabeth gave Jenny a knowing look. She'd guessed this would happen. That was why Elizabeth had been so insistent on Jenny eating lunch here.

She needed to be here, to sit with the team… with this family.

But regardless, Jenny still felt the intrusion, still felt that it was wrong, that she shouldn't be here.

Lacey mentioned the attack on Jenny outside the girls' bathroom, which raised another round of laughter from the team—except for Alice who shot murder at Jenny.

At least she knew where Alice stood.

"You don't need to worry about them anymore," Lacey said. "You're one of us now, even if I don't like it. But anyway, it shouldn't be a problem."

Jenny glared at her sandwich, suddenly feeling like she wasn't hungry anymore. "Maybe not. But the real problem is I never actually asked Jason to that stupid dance."

Lacey grinned. A grin that was nothing but all teeth. "Keep that attitude up and maybe I'll decide you do belong here."

"Thanks, sis. But she asked and I said yes."

Lacey snorted. "Little lady there doesn't seem to think so and I'll bet she'd chose to be friends with us over friends with you."

Jason merely smiled. "You sure about that?"

Great. Just great. Jenny buried her head in her hands. The last team Jenny belonged on was one where a giant like Lacey wanted to be her friend.

TWENTY

Jenny survived lunch. Barely. She also survived changing into her uniform (though only because she changed in the bathroom and not the locker room). Still, when she showed up for the van to take them to the game, more than a few players were surprised to see her.

Alice more than anyone. "Didn't chicken out, huh?"

Jenny just smiled. "And miss getting out of school early? Not on your life. Even if I was *only* sitting on the bench, I'd take up *that* offer."

Alice clenched her fists. "Whatever. You'll be bench-warming for the rest of the season. I promise."

For whatever reason, the other girls didn't jump to Alice's defense. It could have had something to do with Elizabeth, who'd slowly crept her way closer to Jenny's side or it could have been Coach Steele's glare as she slid open the side door. But even though the team didn't *say* anything against Jenny, she felt it.

She wasn't welcome here. They didn't want her.

All that bonding and teasing that had happened over lunch was gone, like the whole thing was something she'd made up.

Jenny took a deep breath, settling the mix of anger and nerves.

Baiting Alice wouldn't help her, not now. She'd need to keep her head on, keep her cool, if she wanted to outwit her dad and his plans for her.

She could do this.

Jenny heard the rumbling of Chuck's truck coming up the school drive. She winced. Between Elizabeth's pestering and lunch, she'd forgotten about Chuck, forgotten he'd be coming.

She hadn't talked to him since that day with the article, had managed to get out of her 'extra' practices because of all the excitement of being on a new team.

She couldn't avoid him forever. But she could, however, avoid him for another day or two.

Jenny filed in behind Alice. For a moment, Alice didn't move, but then with a loud sigh, she scooted over—and happened to 'let' Jenny sit on the seat crack with the stuffing spilling out.

"Just don't touch me." Alice held up Jenny's seat belt.

Jenny hesitated, then accepted the belt.

"What?" Alice shrugged. "I'd hate to see you go through the window or something."

The van quieted.

Elizabeth's head snapped back towards them, lips pressed together. She didn't say anything.

Jenny simply nodded her thanks and buckled up. She had no idea what the hell that was about, but she didn't really care.

She had enough problems on her plate, the least of which being she still had no plan for how to get kicked off the team.

———

In truth, this really was one hell of a team. The way they moved together, thought together, it was like they were one single body and not a dozen different girls with very different (often unique) personalities. And yet, it worked. They made it work.

It took only one inning for her to see that, and by the fifth she'd stopped being surprised at how well they simply worked together. They really were a Goddamn team, a family.

Unlike her who was just floating on the outskirts.

Jenny jogged in from the field, wiping the sweat from her eyes. She'd struck out another two batters—making her total eight for the game—and she felt great.

Alive.

Excited.

She shouldn't feel that way.

The other eight players streamed in behind her. One or two even slapped Jenny on the shoulder, saying 'Good job.'

It was... stunning. That was the only way to describe it. Who'd have thought that by playing well she was already wearing away at their initial hatred of her.

Of course, from her spot on the bench Elizabeth gave Jenny a smile saying she'd known this would happen. And yet... Jenny already felt the shift as the team slowly opened up to her.

But was this what she wanted? Really?

After all, Jenny had been down this road many times. When a team realized Jenny was an asset, they welcomed her in—after all, everyone *wanted* to win. And yet, somewhere along the way Jenny's presence changed the team's dynamics. The competition picked up, tensions spiked. Usually it had something to do with her father, some polite inquiry about a college scout coming to a game.

It would happen again.

It was already starting.

Jenny watched Alice the inning before, who'd warmed up her pitches on the side at Steele's request. Alice was throwing harder, was more intense and focused.

The change, the tension, might be starting with Alice, but it would soon spill over onto the rest of the team. Given enough time, with enough pressure and motivation, it would touch everyone. Even Miss Sunshine Elizabeth.

Alice, who was now slumped forward on the bench, kicked a ball against the fence and it slowly rolled back. "I guess you don't suck out there."

"Yeah, I guess not."

"You know I'm ready to relieve you whenever you need to powder your nose or pose for the cameras."

"Cameras?" Jenny reached for her helmet and paused. "What cameras?"

Alice waved a hand behind her. Sure enough, talking with both Chuck and her mom, was a reporter. Focused, determined, and not a little bit of a cheating sparkle in the eye—this one was no different than the rest. Other than… younger. Like just grown some facial hair younger.

Jenny grabbed her helmet. She was third at bat this inning. She needed to focus. "Probably assigned the crap job because of Dad's stupid article."

The rest of the team drank water, wiped sweat from their foreheads, or ripped open sunflower seed bags. No one but Alice noticed the reporter waiting in the background.

"I thought you'd be pleased," Alice sneered, "he's here for you after all."

Jenny slammed her helmet on her head. "Do I look pleased?"

The sharpness in her voice made Alice sit up straighter, puff out her chest.

Whatever.

"Look," Jenny said, "I'm not getting into a fight with you about this. You don't know anything about me, my life, or whether I even give a damn about having my picture in the newspaper. For your information, I hate reporters, I hate fame, and I'd really like you and everyone who thinks I'm someone special to leave me alone."

Her words rang through the dugout. The team quieted and turned to her. Jenny swallowed a growl, grabbed her bat (*not* the one her dad had given her) and stomped onto the field to get a few swings in before the inning started.

Alice didn't know anything. None of them did. She was damn tired of people making assumptions about her and treating her like shit. Her life had enough crap problems without adding their issues on top of it.

Jenny would go up to bat. She'd put the reporter, her dad, and Alice in the back of her mind. She'd do her job.

She'd also refuse to comment when the reporter came to see her after the game.

So, that's exactly what she did.

She smacked a line drive into right field, which brought in Mandy who scored from third base. The winning run, actually, and the reporter —as expected—used that as the lead-off question when he cornered her the second Jenny left the dugout.

His pimply face looked even more like a mine field up close as he practically pressed his notebook at her. "Another winning hit for you, Miss Taylor. It looked like your dad hadn't exaggerated when he said you had the 'Taylor Bat.'"

Jenny stood there, back tense, clutching her bat bag strap and wanted to snap out the worst reply she could—like telling him and his pimply face to shove it. But that would just piss off her dad and give the reporter a lovely little sound bite.

Either she acted like a bitch and shut him down, or she gave him— and her dad—what they wanted.

"If she *had* the 'Taylor Bat,'" Alice nudged Jenny aside (more closer to shoved, actually), "then she'd have hit a home run and pranced across the plate wearing ballerina slippers."

Alice was helping her?

Jenny's mouth fell open and she nearly dropped her bag on the ground.

The reporter fumbled with his notebook. "And you are, uh…?"

"Someone not nearly important enough for your article. Come on, Jenny, quit hyping up your own fame. You didn't play *that* good." Alice gave her another good shove.

Alice? The girl who tossed frog guts at her had just saved her from a reporter?

What the hell?

TWENTY-ONE

Other than the strange blurp in personality from Alice, the rest of the day progressed as expected. Even Lacey managed a threat about not screwing up the game today (of course, she said this *after* congratulating Jenny). Such was the volatile nature of teenage girls and Jenny just took both the complement, and the threat, in stride.

But team dynamics aside, it was the reporter who Jenny couldn't stop thinking about. Even as Coach Steele had the girls sitting in the outfield grass for the apparently usual after-game team meeting, Jenny found herself drifting.

The reporter had finally left, though he'd successfully managed to chat with Steele for a minute or two.

What had she said? Would Jenny see the article in the paper tomorrow praising her as the new star of Sunny View?

Her stomach rolled. She grabbed a handful of grass, digging her fingers into the dirt. She needed to forget it—forget the reporter and what he'd write. It didn't matter. She was the only one who had control over her life.

Wasn't she?

Later that night, her dad missed dinner again, but when the phone rang her mom bustled across the dinner table to get it. Jenny then had to sit there and listen to a complete recap of the game and how wonderful she'd played.

Jenny speared her green beans with a fork, then flopped the over-cooked vegetable back to the table. Actually, Chuck had already told her dad everything (she'd spotted him on the phone as she got back into the bus). This call was just for Jenny.

About the reporter.

About the interview. *That's* what her dad wanted to know about, not about the game.

Sure enough, when the phone was pushed into Jenny's unresponsive hand, it was the first question out of her dad's mouth.

"So, Jen, how'd it go? Did you give the reporter a good interview?"

"No."

There was a pause on the other line. Jenny continued to spear and unspear the green beans.

"Jennifer."

Quiet. Controlled. Pissed.

"There was a team meeting," she said. "I didn't have time and there was *nothing* to say. I hit the ball. It won the game, but let's not forget the other seven innings the whole team played."

"Jennifer, that's not what —"

"You know, Dad, I gotta go. I have homework."

Jenny jumped from her seat, tossed the phone to her mom, and stomped upstairs. She wasn't going to talk to any damn reporters. Not now, not ever.

She grabbed her backpack from her office chair and dumped the contents onto her bed. She'd lose herself in textbooks and homework. At least school didn't give a shit about her famous dad. Grades were the one thing he couldn't touch, that he couldn't warp.

"I'm not actually someone special," she whispered. And neither was softball special. Her dad was the star, the famous guy. Not her.

Right. As if she believed she'd get away with it that easily.

Not to mention Opening Day was tomorrow and the clubhouse would be overflowing with reporters.

"But they're not there to talk to you."

They'd have their eyes on the famous baseball players. Not on Jenny.

<hr>

OPENING DAY WAS A BIG DAY. For players, for fans, for the media.

Jenny stood outside the open double doors in worn out jeans and the most wrinkled t-shirt she could find. The loud, rolling sounds of the clubhouse swept past her. She hated Opening Day. Hated the man inside, waiting for his family to show up, to stand beside him with that famous smile of his and his sparkling white teeth.

"Come on, Jenny." Her mom nudged her forward. "Don't be shy. How many times have we done this already?"

"You mean with a whole new team and a whole new clubhouse?"

"That's enough, Jenny. You already said enough last night to your father. Be happy he still wanted you here."

"We won't even talk about what I want," Jenny muttered.

"I'll pretend like I didn't hear that. And besides, you wore that horrid outfit like you wanted."

Only because Jenny refused to step outside if her mom had foisted her into something actually nice and flattering.

"Now come on; we're late."

Late was fine by her.

The sharp smell of recently shampooed carpet from the lounge and locker rooms drifted in the air, barely hiding the sweat and dirt which had soaked into the walls and floor after so many years. No one but Jenny seemed to notice the smell, how it settled in the back of her throat and made her want to gag.

Jenny lost the battle of wills against her mother (as if she'd had a chance) and descended into the world of glitz and cameras, baseballs and bats. A world, by the way, that had its fair share of beautiful women and trophy wives.

Her mom, in a snug purple dress that flowed down her hips, with the tiny sprinkling of diamonds in her ears, looked like she was born to be here. Born to be in the spotlight of the clubhouse.

The perfect, self-contained, self-controlled woman the world expected to see on Sam Taylor's arm.

Not, of course, the woman the media expected to see him kissing all over the tabloids, but so long as he had the appearance of a stable, supportive family… well, some bits of his life could be 'overlooked' by the fans and eaten up by starving, underfed hyenas (meaning the press).

But thankfully, none of *those* women were present. Not on Opening Day, not when it was a day for the families.

Her dad was in the thick of it, charming and smiling like always. Standing tall in his newly pressed suit, shaking hands with kids, wives, and the media. The media was always present in the clubhouse and her dad knew each by name within 24 hours of settling onto a new team.

Because of school, Jenny and her mom weren't as early as they normally were, but her dad didn't seem to notice. In fact, he never once glanced in their direction.

"Now don't you wish you'd brought a friend?" Her mom whispered into Jenny's ear so she could hear.

"No."

Her mom made a loud, expected sigh. "Behave yourself, will you? And can you at least pretend like you're happy to be here?"

Jenny shrugged, then made her way through the dense crowd of people, trying to not jar anyone too famous and knock beer onto their expensive shirts.

Last time that happened her dad had grounded her for a month. How was she *supposed* to know the guy with his bulging stomach was the team owner?

Still, everything was what Jenny expected.

Just as she expected her dad to be talking to the hot-body reporter in the off-pink suit and cleavage displayed as her number-one asset. Oh, and her media badge happened to land just perfectly between those sculpted breasts.

He laughed at something Size Double-D said and clapped his fellow player, Cly Stanly, on the shoulder. Cly barely came up to her dad's chin so the poor guy shook with the force, but he seemed to have a perfect view of the reporters… 'badge.'

Yep. Her dad definitely knew *this* reporter.

Jenny wove her way through the purple and gold shirts, colors worn to support the team, and kept her attention on the constantly moving bodies as she made her way to the snack table with its obligatory cheese, crackers, fruit—and of course, cookies.

Reporters, players, and families occupied every space to the point the 'Chargers' symbol on the carpet was almost completely covered up. Even a throng of kids had set up a tower of Lego's in the far corner.

Just another day at the ball park.

At least the cookies would be good.

Jenny snatched a napkin and reached for the biggest cookie, one that also happened to be loaded with chocolate chips.

"Hello," a woman said behind her, "you must be Sam Taylor's daughter."

Jenny glanced over her shoulder as Double-D came up behind her. Her hand slowly dropped away from the cookie, just as her stomach dropped to the floor.

"I'm Samantha Dawson from *The Sunny View Gazette.*" She held out her hand. "And I'd love to do an interview with you."

Jenny stood there, frozen. Her heart thundered in her chest. Why did she want to talk to *Jenny?* She was no one, completely unimportant.

But why did the reporter's name sound so familiar?

TWENTY-TWO

This was sooo not happening.

Jenny scanned the room, searching for her dad, her mom—anyone that could save her. They were gone.

She was surrounded by strangers. She didn't even recognize any of the Chargers players who were still at the party. The game must be closer to starting than she'd realized.

Samantha still stood there, hand outstretched, but Jenny made no move to take it.

"You know the person you should really talk to is my dad. He's around here." Somewhere. Where was he when she actually *wanted* him?

"Oh, that's quite all right. I already did. He suggested I speak with you. Directly."

Shit.

Why did this woman want to talk with Jenny? She was a nobody.

For instance, the room was filled with a bunch of nobody family members. How come they weren't being harassed by a reporter who could smother them with her boobs?

"You know, I've got to be going —" Jenny moved around Samantha, but Double-D was ready for her.

"Oh! These cookies look delicious." Samantha reached for the cookie tray, blocking Jenny. She was now trapped between Double-D and the cookie tray.

To make matters worse the damn bitch had to grab the cookie that Jenny had been eying.

"Excellent," Samantha purred as she took a bite. "I love a good chocolate chip cookie and the Chargers cook is amazing. You should have one."

"No thanks."

All Jenny wanted was to get the hell out of there, but there was still no sign of her mom. Crap. Maybe she *should* have brought a friend. Someone who could have easily stepped in and saved her.

But there was no such person. Not here. Not in her world.

Samantha licked a smudge of chocolate off her finger. If her dad had been here Jenny was sure he'd be licking his lips and getting ready to have Samantha for dessert.

Anger swelled up inside Jenny, pushing aside her hesitation. The only reason she was in this mess was because of her dad.

"Now why don't we spend a few moments getting to know each other?" Samantha asked.

"I can't think of any reason why we should."

"How about your father and all those great comments he made about you? You remember, don't you? I'm sure you read my article."

Holy crap. The article. That's why Samantha's name was so familiar.

"I also sent one of my little interns to the game, but he didn't have a chance to talk with you. I'm hoping to correct that." Samantha leaned in and Jenny pressed herself against the table.

The table wobbled but didn't fall.

"I'd especially like to know your plans for playing professional softball."

"I, I mean there's nothing...."

"What was that, dear?" Like a weasel scenting a wounded prey, Samantha slipped out a notebook from her suit (from where exactly, Jenny didn't have a damn clue). She clicked open her pen and poised it above the paper. "You do want to play softball, don't you? Follow in your father's steps? Continue with the 'Taylor Legacy,' as he calls it?"

Sweat beaded Jenny's forehead. She grabbed the table cloth and squeezed. What was she going to do?

"There you are!" A loud, angry, and not nice voice jumped from behind Double-D. It was a voice Jenny recognized. And dreaded.

Alice? What the hell was Alice doing here?

"Damn, Jenny, I've been looking for you everywhere." Alice pushed her way through the crowd, looking mad as all hell with her high-swinging ponytail—which also managed to smack some poor kid's face when he didn't move fast enough.

Unlike Alice's usual off-the-shoulder shirts with a smattering of holes dotted along the collar, she'd upscaled. Now it was an off-the-shoulder shirt with no holes and jeans that were so low it looked like they'd fall off any minute. But there was no mistaking her glare—a glare that was now directed at Samantha.

Double-D whirled around on her four inch pumps, but didn't put away her notebook. Or her pen. "Oh. Hello. Jennifer, is this one of your friends?"

"Teammate," Alice snapped.

She didn't say friend. That was fine since they technically weren't and never would be, friends.

Still—why the hell was Alice here?

"Excellent." Samantha backed off slightly from Jenny, but she was still close enough to pin her if needed.

Jenny would have to be quick to get by. That was fine. She was quick and now with Alice helping to distract Samantha....

"I would love to get your opinion on Jennifer," Samantha said. "You attend the same high school, correct? Your team isn't doing so well this season are you? And with so many seniors graduating and this being their last shot at the championship —"

"If you want to talk about the seniors, interview them." Alice whipped her head towards Jenny, which caused that deadly ponytail of hers to whip at Samantha's face.

The reporter pulled back just in time.

"Jenny. Your mom's looking for you."

Hell, she'd take whatever help she could get right now. Even if it was from Alice. "Thanks. Best not keep her waiting. Nice to meet you Ms. Dawson."

Bullshit.

"One more quick question, Jennifer." Samantha shoved her hips at Jenny, but she was ready this time.

Ready and mad.

"You know, Ms. Dawson, I'm not eighteen right?"

Samantha blinked, then her lips curved into a slow smile. "Yes, but as I explained I've already gotten your father's consent —"

By some weird act of God, Alice knew exactly where Jenny was going. "Except he's not present, dumbass. Which means you're not allowed to talk to her. Now move your cleavage before I run you over."

Samantha's mouth dropped. A laugh bubbled up Jenny's throat. She held it in though, somehow managing to swallow it. No point letting Alice know just how grateful she was.

The other pitcher would probably use it as ammo against her.

Jenny dodged Samantha again—grabbing two giant cookies from the tray—and gave one to Alice. Alice paused to look at the cookie, then at Jenny. She shrugged and took a bite. Jenny did the same.

They lost themselves in the thick of the crowd, but Jenny was finished with being here. With baseball.

They made their way to a quieter corner, the one now abandoned by the kids who'd been playing Lego's. They'd left the scattered pieces on the smelly carpet.

Fumes probably got to them.

"You mind telling me what you're doing here?" Jenny took another bite of her cookie.

"Don't get any ideas. It's not because I like you." Alice finished off the rest and said with her mouth still full, "I came to save you."

TWENTY-THREE

Save her? Jenny nearly dropped her half-eaten cookie. "What are you... I mean, how could you...."

Alice rubbed her hands and dropped crumbs onto the Lego's. "Don't get all choked up. I didn't want to come."

"No. Of course not." Jenny's head spun. None of this was making sense. "But why are you here?"

"Elizabeth. The team. Freakin' Laurie, too. She's the one who said if I wanted to pitch this summer I'd better get my ass to the ballpark. Oh, and she had Jack call to get my name on the guest list, so I guess the guy still has connections. Like I care. I did my job." Alice pushed off the wall. "Well, are you coming?"

Coming? Jenny's gaze swept over the slowly emptying clubhouse, but while the families might be leaving, the reporters didn't seem to be. The players would soon be 'closed for comment' until after the game.

Which meant Samantha would have another clean shot at Jenny.

"Sure. Okay." Jenny wiped her own crumbs on her jeans. "Where are we going? I mean, I didn't realize you were old enough to drive."

Alice scowled, tossed her ponytail over her shoulder—nearly whacking Jenny in the process—and walked out of the clubhouse. Jenny stared after her, unsure if she should follow. She was safe from

Samantha, at least for now. She could make her way to the box seats where her mom and other families were waiting. That's what she *should* do.

Or she could follow Alice.

Jenny straightened, shoving her shoulders back. She'd have to face her mom—and her dad learning about her again ditching a reporter—soon enough. What was wrong with a little fun? And if the team had actually sent Alice to 'save' Jenny… well, maybe she should just see what this was all about.

Since Alice wasn't old enough to drive, Jenny wasn't surprised to see Elizabeth leaning out of some steel monstrosity. "I see Alice found you."

Jenny stopped a few paces away from the car even as Alice crawled into the passenger seat. Still unsure, still hesitant, Jenny glanced back once at the open stadium doors.

"You coming?" Elizabeth asked.

She didn't know. "Where are you going?"

"To the best pizza place in town. You been to *Joe's* yet?"

"No. I haven't."

"Well, okay then. Hop in."

Jenny didn't know if she'd still be standing there if it hadn't been for Alice. It was like Alice was her evil twin who knew exactly which button of Jenny's to push (or in some cases slam with repeated, unnecessary force until Jenny fumed from the ears).

It was a good thing Elizabeth was driving. Otherwise, Jenny wasn't sure they'd have arrived in one piece.

Jenny called her mom to let her know what was up, and after some slight hysteria (apparently her mom hadn't realized Jenny was missing), she calmed down. After all, she was eating with the softball team, and her mom's, "Okay, dear. Just don't be out late," said everything—as in—thank God my daughter's finally making friends.

Except she wasn't.

After all, this was only pizza. It was nothing special. That's what Jenny told herself until Elizabeth ushered her into *Joe's*, with its wood-shaving floors, mile-high pitchers of beer, and the tangy smells of tomato sauce, wood-fired bread, and sizzling sausage.

Within seconds Jenny's mouth was coated in saliva. "My God, this place smells amazing."

"Gee. Imagine what it tastes like." Alice shoved past her, but the place smelled so good Jenny didn't care—or shove her back.

Elizabeth merely shook her head and told Jenny to come on. They went to a back table, nearest to the vintage, quarter-operated arcade games, except the table Alice selected was already occupied. With two other members of the team: Mandy, the catcher from yesterday's game, and Lacey.

Jenny swallowed, suddenly very unsure about her rather impromptu decision to ditch her dad's game, when Elizabeth gave her a slight nudge.

"It's all right. Trust me."

Trust. The one thing Jenny had forgotten in the years of moving, of changing schools and teams as quickly as she changed socks. But what else could she do?

"Well," Lacey drawled as she slid across the blood-red cushioned seat, "look who decided to show up?"

"I hope you like meat," Mandy said, "we already ordered."

"Uh, yeah," Jenny managed. "Meat's fine."

What was going on? Had Elizabeth planned this?

Alice waited long enough to demand a diet Coke from the waitress, then whipped out her iPhone and started texting, completely ignoring Jenny and the others. This was fine. Dealing with one girl who hated her was bad enough. Throw in both Lacey and Alice—Jenny doubted even she could survive dinner, regardless of how great the pizza smelled.

Jenny shifted in her seat. "How did you know I'd need help?"

Elizabeth shrugged. "It seemed like a fair enough assumption, especially after that article and the reporter at the game."

Jenny's face paled. "You saw that, huh?"

Lacey snorted. "We're not stupid. Jason kept the guy off you while you changed cleats until your buddy Chuck took charge."

Jenny tensed at Chuck's name. The girls paused in their talking, as if waiting for an explanation.

"I'm mad at him right now." Jenny fiddled with a napkin. "He knew what Dad was doing and he… he didn't tell me."

"Yeah," Elizabeth said, "we know how that goes around here."

"Especially Elizabeth," Lacey added. "You're not the only one with a famous dad."

Jenny knew. If only hers had been the one to walk away from baseball instead of walking away from her family. This, however, she kept to herself.

She might be eating pizza with them, but that didn't make her part of the team, that didn't make her part of their family. And yet, as quickly as her dad was brought up he was brushed aside. It was like they decided he no longer existed in their universe and therefore weren't allowed to dwell on him.

Instead, Jenny got to hear about the other girls—Elizabeth and her bubbling relationship with a guy named Michael; Lacey, who declared she needed no man, decided instead to rail about her stupid mother. Lacey also mentioned Jason quite a bit—especially how he kept going on about his reluctant date to the dance.

At this, she gave a pointed look at Jenny.

"Don't look at me," Jenny muttered, "I didn't ask him to anything."

All of the girls (except for Alice who'd mumbled something about the bathroom and disappeared) stared at Jenny.

"Riiiight," Lacey said, "you just keep thinking that. Either way, he's set on going with you so you better have a dress picked out." She leaned across the table and thumped her plastic knife on the wooden, cracked table. "Because if you're not ready with all the make-up and hair when he answers the door, you and I are going to have a nice chat."

Right. "Yeah, okay."

She'd get out of it first. She had to.

There was no way she was going to any dance with Jason.

And while Jenny slowly found herself relaxing, found her lips curling up in what had to be a smile, it was the pizza that truly did the trick. For as much as Jenny wanted to remain apart, to simply observe these girls and not feel anything… the pizza made her smile.

It was really, really that good.

Heavenly.

It alone broke down her barriers, shattered her reservations.

She moaned as she bit into her third slice. "This is amazing. I'm not going to be able to walk tomorrow, but it's sooo worth it."

The others agreed.

"See?" Elizabeth slid another slice onto Jenny's soaked-through plastic plate. "I told you it was worth it."

And it was. Every minute of it. Even Alice when she accidentally let a smile slip at something Jenny said.

She couldn't help but wonder if this was what it was like to have friends, to have a family.

TWENTY-FOUR

J enny had enjoyed herself.

The thought shook her as Elizabeth dropped her off at her parents' house. Even when she unlocked the front door, the surprise was still there. It vibrated through her with each passing second and she still couldn't believe it.

Didn't believe it.

"Jenny," her mother called from the living room. "Your father —"

She stopped when she saw Jenny, still standing in the foyer, hand on the doorknob. "You know what? Never mind. He'll talk to you after tomorrow's game. You had a good time?"

"Yeah."

Her mom wanted more details and Jenny knew she wouldn't leave until she heard something good. So, she told her mom about *Joe's* pizza and the arcade game she'd played for a couple of rounds.

She didn't mention she'd been playing with Alice. Okay, they hadn't been playing 'together' but they weren't actually trying to kill each other—just the hordes of undead.

It was enough for her mom and she left Jenny for the rest of the night. She didn't ask why Jenny had bolted from the clubhouse, but Jenny figured she was pleased to look the other way and concentrate on the good things. Meaning Jenny having friends, which she mentioned several times.

"I knew it would happen. I knew Sunny View was the place for us."

In fact, come Saturday morning—and then Saturday afternoon—her mom was still saying the same thing. And truthfully, Jenny was enjoying spending time with her mom. For once neither of them were worried about her dad, though he was always in the back of Jenny's mind, a silent threat.

He'd be home soon enough. But there was no sense worrying about what he'd say when she already knew.

Still, they'd planned on going back to *Joe's* for dinner and her mom was just reaching for her car keys when Dad roared up the driveway. Her mom's hand paused inches from the keys. "It looks like your dad's home."

Jenny's good mood faded. She'd known it wouldn't last, couldn't last.

"Jenny, I can —"

"Forget it, Mom." He'd say what he wanted to say, which was only what Sam Taylor cared about. Jenny dropped her purse on the glass coffee table and settled into the seat to wait. She didn't wait long.

There was no denying the fury in her dad, the way it rolled off him and soaked the room. He didn't slam the door closed. That wasn't his way. Instead, he stepped into his house, slow and deliberate, then quietly shut the door behind him.

The click echoed through the room.

"Sam," her mom's voice wavered as she reached for him. "Jenny and I were just going to get pizza. Would you like to come?"

"Jenny and I," he growled, "are going to have a discussion. Right now."

A discussion. There would be no 'discussion' about it. Not when it was his way only; not when he didn't give a shit about what she wanted.

"Imagine my surprise that after months of my careful hard work of getting her into the spotlight that she throws it all back in my face. Did you think I wouldn't find out? That Samantha wouldn't tell me?"

Oh, Samantha had told him all right. Probably over black satin sheets while they sipped wine.

"Sam?" her mom echoed. "What are you talking about?"

With the same deliberate slowness, Jenny got to her feet. "Clearly, Mom, while Dad told you he was mad he forgot to mention that little detail about being mad about me not talking to a reporter."

She crossed her arms. "Okay, Dad. Let's *discuss* this. How could you do that to me? How could you let her trap me? I was alone. Alone! How could you do that?"

"It's the media," he snapped. "You need to get used to it."

"No, I don't." Jenny balled her fists. She wanted to scream and stomp, anything to get through the incredibly dense, selfish head of his! "You're the one who's playing professional ball. Not me. You deal with the media. I'm still in high school."

"You won't always be!" Her dad's hold on his temper frayed. His passion sparked through, merging with his anger. This was the man who'd worked for years to play for the Major Leagues, who'd willingly sacrificed himself, his family, all in the name of success.

Jenny backed up a step. Her legs smacked into the sofa. "I'm not you and I'm never going to be you."

Her mom placed a calming hand on his arm, but it didn't work. Not the way it used to.

He simply shrugged her off. "She's not a child anymore and I refuse to let her ruin her future."

But for once, her mom didn't back off. "Sam. She's sixteen. She can't talk to a reporter, not by herself and certainly not without telling me."

"We have to move quickly on this. If we have a shot at not only getting Jenny into professional ball, but the kind of money backing the league needs, we need to start early. As far as I'm concerned, we should have started the second she picked up a ball."

Jenny paled. So did her mother.

That was what finally got through to her dad. Not Jenny's yelling, but her mom's pale face, her shaking hand as she picked up her keys and slipped her purse on her shoulder.

"Carol," he whispered, "that's not what I meant."

"Yes, it was."

"Look. I'm doing this for Jenny, for *her.* We need people to start thinking about her, to start paying attention to her. It's the only way to get her name—*our* name—out there."

"Your name, you mean." Her mom turned to Jenny. "Get your coat. You promised me pizza."

It was the first time Jenny had ever seen her mom stand up to her dad. It was enough to make even Jenny's breath come in short, jagged gasps. Even when she got to the car, neither hers or her mom's hands had stopped shaking.

"He's not going to let this drop is he?" Jenny asked.

"No, dear. He's not. He wants what's best for you."

"You mean what's best for him."

Her mom started the car and said nothing. Apparently this was as far over the line as she could cross against her husband.

That meant the rest was up to Jenny.

TWENTY-FIVE

Jenny stared at her sagging sandwich and wanted to throw up. It wasn't the sandwich's fault. The feeling hadn't left her since the argument with her dad two days ago.

A feeling which had even successfully ruined the amazing *Joe's* pizza.

And now, with a game in a few hours and her starting as second baseman while Alice took the mound, Jenny needed the energy of food. The problem was she doubted she'd keep it down for an hour.

"What the hell are you doin' here, Transfer?" Lacey booted Jenny's back with her foot and pushed. "You think I'm gonna search for you every damn game?"

"Lacey? What are you…?"

"Get up. Whether I like it or not, you're on the team. Therefore you eat with the team."

Jenny was apparently not moving fast enough for Lacey, who snatched up Jenny's backpack and left her to catch up.

What Jenny had wanted was to be left alone. Right now, she couldn't deal with a bunch of girls like Alice who didn't want her there.

The team sat in their usual spot underneath the tree. Jenny freed her backpack from Lacey's clutches and looked for Jason. For some reason she needed to see his smile, needed some reassurance that her life... well it didn't truly suck.

But maybe it did, because he wasn't there.

As if Lacey knew who she was looking for, she plopped onto the bench beside Jenny. "Looking for your boyfriend?"

"No. And he's not my boyfriend."

"Right. I'll be sure to tell him that." Lacey took a burger and fries from Mandy, who must have gotten it from the cafeteria.

"You know that'll probably kill you?" Jenny gagged at the smell of not-real meat.

"Breakfast of champions." Lacey proceeded to demolish the burger. Jenny had to look away.

Now she really wanted to throw up.

The other girls weren't paying much attention, including Elizabeth whose nose was in a book nearly the size of her.

"He's helping the guys," Lacey said in between bites of meat—which swirled around her half-open mouth.

"Guys?" Even with the disgusting sight of Lacey eating, Jenny couldn't help but ask.

"The baseball team. They're playing Mount Crest tomorrow—a team about as good as their softball team. Jason's giving their freshman ace some help. And speaking of Mount Crest, bring your uniform tomorrow, too. We always support the guys against Mount Crest."

Great. Another day with the team.

Still, Jenny eased into the bench and realized Lacey had given her the perfect opening. "So Jason *did* play baseball. I mean, he's said as much but didn't —"

Lacey froze her words with a look, then went back to her burger. "He doesn't play anymore and you'd best just drop it. He's helping his old team out, that's all."

But it was more than Lacey's not-so-subtle threat that made Jenny sit up and take notice. Lacey, Jenny saw, carefully avoided looking not at Jenny, but at Alice. Alice who'd gone just as tense as the last time someone mentioned Jason around her.

They *must* have been dating. It had to have ended badly.

But Alice and Jason couldn't have anything to do with him playing baseball, especially how everyone refused to talk about it.

Maybe… maybe she could do some of her own research, just like she'd done with the softball team. After all, a small internet search for Jason Richards would tell her something.

Jenny worried her lower lip. Except wouldn't she be breaking his privacy? Didn't she hate it when people did that with her?

Best leave both Alice and Jason alone because right now, Jenny needed to do something about her dad, especially since she was on her own. No Chuck, no mom to back her up.

She was alone. But that was okay. She was used to being alone. And no matter what happened, she'd get herself through it.

She always did.

But what could she do? She was sixteen and had no say in her life. Maybe she did need help, at least a little advice.

Not from the team, though, and definitely not from Jason.

Jenny took a small bite of her sandwich. Maybe it was time to talk with Chuck. If she could trust him.

She just didn't know if she could.

TWENTY-SIX

For the team's second game against Skyline in the season, they were at the top of their game. Not Jenny so much. She still managed a few hits, got in a run or two, but her spark was gone. The zing of playing, of fielding a ball and nearly making a double play, vanished.

Instead it left behind an empty hollowness.

She and Heather, the senior short stop, had almost made a double-play happen, but Jenny had thrown the ball slightly too high, making Heather reach a little too far. The throw offset Heather's balance enough that they didn't make the out on first.

The runner was called safe.

Groans echoed from the stands, disappointment the play hadn't worked, but still caught up in the excitement.

From the stands she noticed Chuck and Jason watching in silence. Neither of them cheered. Both studied her, faces revealing nothing.

She was distracted, not much, but enough to make a difference and they knew it. They could see it.

Chuck made sense, but Jason? How could he know her that well? He couldn't!

Softball usually got Jenny's mind off things—but not this time. Not when softball was at the heart of her problems. At least there were no reporters. That was one good thing.

As she tossed her glove onto the bench, Jenny glanced at Chuck who clutched his baseball hat in his hands. Usually Chuck was Mr. Intense. He was totally focused on Jenny and the other team. He'd pass on tips he'd see from the other pitcher or some mistake the rival coach had missed about their team's weakness.

Not this time.

His head was bowed and he just kept crushing his Chargers hat over and over again.

Elizabeth slid onto the bench beside Jenny. She hadn't pitched yet this season, but if it bothered her she didn't let it show. Jenny admired that about her, how she always had a smile on.

But sometimes she hated that smile. Like now when the last thing Jenny wanted was to smile.

"You two still not talking?"

"Ah, no." She pulled her gaze away from Chuck.

But she needed too. Soon. They needed to talk because as much as Jenny didn't want help… she did.

And no one knew her dad better than Chuck.

"You never said how things went," Elizabeth said. "After Opening Day."

There'd been a reason. "My mom was cool. Happy, actually that I'm finally 'making friends'."

The friends comment slipped out, which only made Elizabeth's smile widen and Jenny's stomach churn. She didn't have any friends. This team *wasn't* her friend.

"And your dad?"

"It came up once."

And that was all she was going to say. If there was anyone who could understand, it was Elizabeth, but Jenny just wasn't ready—just couldn't tell the other girl (the luckier girl in her mind) what he'd said, what he would *do* to see his legacy carried on.

"And…?" Elizabeth asked.

"And we talked. It didn't go well."

The sunshine that was Elizabeth dimmed, but only slightly. "You know, Jenny, you can talk to me."

"No. I can't."

From the end of the dugout, Alice shot Jenny a glare as she shoved her helmet on, then blew her a rather rude kiss.

No one on the team missed it.

No one said anything either.

But really, this was the last freakin' thing Jenny needed to deal with right now. Everything piled on. From trusting Chuck, from her dad and his stupid legacy plans, to Elizabeth pushing her when she clearly did *not* want to talk about it —

She'd had enough.

"Why the hell does she hate me?"

Elizabeth fiddled with the ends of her braids. "It's not you."

"You sure about that? Because I'm pretty sure I'm the only one she's throwing kissy faces at."

The image of Jason sitting beside her on the grass, his legs lightly brushing hers, feeling the coarse fabric of his jeans on her bare skin, punched her in the gut. Stole her breath. "Is it Jason? Were they a, you know...?"

"Jason? Oh, no. It's not that. They aren't a couple. Were never a couple. It's not like that."

Relief swept into Jenny's gut, right behind that damn punch. She absolutely refused to think about either because she didn't think of Jason like that. There was no way in hell she *liked* him.

Now only if her stupid stomach and that spark would get in line with her head, she'd be fine.

"So," Jenny said, "then she just hates me for the hell of it?"

"It's complicated."

"It always is." Especially with girls. That's why the guys had it easier. They got paid the big bucks of baseball *and* they didn't have to deal with girl-drama. "So she hates me because I moved her lower in the pitcher rotation?"

"It's not that." Elizabeth dropped her braids and lowered her voice, leaned in so the others couldn't easily overhear. Not that this was difficult since they were cheering Alice as she went to bat. "Okay, that's some of it, but not all. It's your type. Your softball type. You're focused, intense, determined. She looks at you and knows you're going all the way to the top."

Elizabeth smirked. "The newspaper didn't get that wrong about you. What they did get wrong was that in the end, it's your choice."

The vomiting feeling came back full force. "This isn't about me."

"Yes, it is. You remind Alice of her brother and the accident...." Elizabeth's mouth clamped shut. "I'm sorry. I shouldn't say anything. I just wanted to let you know it's nothing personal. If you stick around long enough she'll warm up to you. Promise."

That wasn't the kind of reassurance Jenny needed. What she needed was answers. Answers to Alice, to Jason and his mysterious interest, answers to her own life.

And it looked like she wasn't going to get any today, regardless of how badly she wanted them.

So she thought.

At least until Chuck came up to her after the game, face haggard, eyes looking smudged and bruised.

"I asked Coach Steele if I could take you home."

"Great." Even though she needed to talk with him it didn't mean she wanted to.

"We need to talk, Jen."

Her bag felt like lead weight on her arm. In the parking lot, she saw Jason pause before getting into his own car. It was a single hesitation, hardly worth noting, except he *had* hesitated. Hesitated for her.

Seeing this, seeing he still cared about her even though he hadn't said a single word during the game or after, gave Jenny the courage to nod.

Nod both to Jason and Chuck.

"Yeah. I guess we do."

Whatever was coming, she'd face this head on. And maybe once she knew the playing field, maybe once she knew what she was up against with her dad, she could find a way to drive a couple runs of her own in.

She could hope, anyway. She followed Chuck to his truck and he tossed her bag into the open bed. "What are we going to talk about?"

He didn't answer. Not directly.

"Your mom called me Saturday night. She told me about the reporter."

It was the last thing Jenny had expected him to say.

TWENTY-SEVEN

S he did what?" The words whispered out of Jenny. "She called you? She couldn't have."

Impossible. Not after what she'd seen in the car, the way her mom's hands shook, the way she backed away from the problem, afraid to deal with it. Forcing Jenny to take this all on her own.

"She did. Get in the truck. We'll talk on the way."

They didn't, actually, talk. Not on the drive. It was like Chuck could only focus on one thing at a time and driving had his undivided attention, at least until they came in sight of the peach colored monstrosity her dad called a 'house.'

Chuck pulled off to the side of the road and turned off the engine. "I didn't know. I didn't know what he'd been planning. About the reporter, about the sponsorships... about the number of them he'd already contacted."

"You suspected."

Chuck's hands tightened on the steering wheel. "Not this. Never this. I'm sorry. Christ, Jen, I'm sorry. When your mom called, when she told me... I thought it was impossible. I thought she'd been mistaken or you hadn't heard right."

"So you called Dad. You asked him yourself."

Chuck fumbled with his seat belt, got out, and slammed the door behind him.

Jenny followed. "Tell me. What did he say?"

Chuck paced up and down the street. If there'd been cars driving by he would have walked right into them. A good thing there weren't any. She needed answers.

She grabbed his flannel shirt, forced him to stop, to look at her. "Damn it, Chuck! Just tell me."

"Samantha Dawson will personally be attending your big game. The Mount Crest game. He's already talked to Coach Steele. No amount of weaseling or promises worked on her at least, to a degree."

"What, what do you mean?"

"Lacey's still the starting pitcher, but you'll be going in as a relief. Even if Lacey throws the best game of her life, Steele promised your dad you'd pitch."

Jenny's fingers slipped free of his shirt. "He's gotten to her."

"Of course he did. He's got charisma, money. Shit tons of money. He gets to everyone." Chuck turned away from her, stared at the mansion. "Even me."

"You're telling me now." That had to count for something, didn't it?

"Only because he crossed the line."

He faced her, his face looking more worn and wrinkled than she'd ever seen him. It was like he'd aged ten years, the way his shoulders hunched, his back bent. "I let it get this far. I knew what he was doing and I should have stopped it. I didn't."

She didn't blame him, not really. Couldn't. She hadn't stopped her dad either. Neither had her mom. Besides, Jenny had only been a job to him.

"It was your job," she said.

"No job is worth this. Worth pushing a kid to grow up quickly, to force her into a life she doesn't want, and doesn't have a choice in making. I'm not an idiot, Jen. I know you don't want it. I know you don't want to play pro ball. Hell, after what your dad has put you guys through I can't say I blame you."

It was nice to hear him admit it, to hear that he'd known. And more than anything it was nice to hear the apology, the sorrow. And more than anything, she now knew she wasn't alone.

She had a friend. Kind of. Even if this friend's job was still to make her into the best softball player on the planet.

Still, her stomach swished and the urge to vomit had her bending over, hands on her knees. She didn't, thankfully, but she leaned against Chuck's truck and closed her eyes against the pain.

All those of years of training hard, of pitching day in and day out, sometimes two or three times a day. Always to please her dad. She'd thought he'd care more, would be around more if he saw she was becoming his legacy. His heir.

It wasn't enough. It had never been enough.

"When I was younger," she whispered, "I played to get his attention, to make him proud of me."

Chuck gave a half-snort, half-laugh. "Trust me, Jen. He's proud of you. It's twisted and screwed up, but never doubt that he's proud of you."

Something in her heart twisted, bled.

Those words weren't enough for her to believe him, to feel the love her father should have given her without restraint, without ties or conditions attached to it.

"Do you know what he's planning?" she asked.

"I do."

Jenny opened her eyes and faced Chuck. "Tell me."

In the end, he did. And in the end, Jenny found herself bending over into some neighbor's bush, someone who she hadn't yet met, and puking her guts out.

He couldn't. He would. Oh, God, he would.

Chuck was beside her, holding back her hair, his mouth set in a grim line. He'd even fetched her a water bottle and napkin when she'd finished.

Jenny drank the water, then slumped onto the side of the curb, holding her head in between her hands. They were shaking.

"Nike?" she whispered.

"It's on the table. I don't know all the details—or if they even know how young you are."

Her father hadn't been kidding when he'd meant 'starting early.' He wanted the world to know who she was, wanted everyone to know about the Taylor Legacy and how Jenny would change professional softball.

"It's not just the talk either, or getting the word out or the sponsors." Chuck gripped Jenny's shoulder. She didn't look at him. "He's banking a lot of his own money into this too."

She sniffed. "Not enough to stop buying expensive-ass cars."

"No." He paused. "I think he's waiting until your senior year before he gets out the big guns."

Shit.

"What am I going to do? I have to play. He'll make me play. Coach Steele will make me play."

She truly was alone. Lost.

Chuck's grip on her shoulder tightened. "Yes. But you don't have to play well."

Jenny's head jerked up. The breath whooshed out of her. "What?"

"He can make you play, Jen. He can force you on that team or any other, but he can't make you play well. He can't force you to be the softball superstar we all know you are. You're the only one who can do that."

TWENTY-EIGHT

C huck was right.

Her dad had taken everything else away from her, taken away any say she'd ever had in softball, which position she'd play, which teams she'd play for. But Chuck was right.

Her dad couldn't take this from her.

He couldn't force her to push herself, to drive herself, to stand on the mound and pitch with her whole heart.

Jenny wiped the sweat from her forehead as she glanced at Chuck who sat in the stands, still just as quiet as last time, but no less nervous.

Chuck would see it. He would know. He'd taken one look at her, the second her foot touched the mound, and he'd known.

She'd listened to him.

Jenny got the next sign from Mandy, breathed in, soft and quiet, then pitched the curve ball as directed. Rocked back on her heels, arms shooting forward, her right arm wind-milling as she'd done since she turned seven.

She pitched the ball as she'd practiced, her body knowing the motion, the way to snap the ball, to make it curve. Her body went through the motions, but she put nothing behind it.

No oomph. No power. No heart.

The batter got more than just a small piece of the ball. She'd gotten a good chunk. But Lacey was one hell of a third baseman, grabbed the ball in one bounce and threw to first.

The pitch hadn't curved as hard or tight as normal. Jenny hadn't expected it to. She'd felt it, felt the second she'd pitched the ball.

She didn't smile. There was no reason to smile. This might be the only way, the only chance she had at freedom, at making her own choice, but it wasn't anything to be happy about.

Elizabeth, who played first, gave Jenny a slanted look, curious with one eyebrow raised. But she didn't ask the question and instead tossed the ball back to Jenny.

The team was winning. Jenny was playing fine. Not great. But fine.

The one thing Jenny wouldn't do was purposefully throw a game. That wasn't right. Regardless of her dad and his underhanded tactics, she refused to stoop that low.

Still, when she glanced to the stands and caught Chuck's attention, he nodded once. This would have been fine, would have just made her turn and focus back on the task at hand.

The only problem was Jason. Jason, who was sitting to Chuck's right, noticed the nod.

His clear, crystal sharp eyes snapped to Jenny. Held hers. In his eyes he asked the question Elizabeth hadn't been willing to.

Jenny simply stared back, just as hard and just as determined. She gave him his answer.

When the game ended, a close one but the Tigers still edged ahead, Jenny expected Jason to lay into her the first chance he got, demanded to know what the hell she was doing.

He didn't.

He stomped off the field, snapping at anyone who tried to talk with him. As far as Jenny was concerned, she was perfectly fine with that. Even with him stalking off toward the parking lot, Jenny could feel the tension between them. Hard and pulsing, making it harder to breathe.

Whatever. This had nothing to do with him.

She hadn't pitched terribly. They hadn't lost the game. The Tigers would still have a shot at winning the Championship.

She dumped her cleats into her bag and ripped off her knee pads. She hadn't done anything wrong. So why did it feel like she was letting him down? Why did it feel like in some tiny, remote part of her that she was letting him down… both him and the team.

"They're not my team," she muttered quietly. She played for them because she had no choice. That was the whole point.

Alice, whose bag had gotten dumped next to Jenny's, snatched it up. "What the hell did you do this time to get him mad?"

"I have no idea what you're talking about."

Alice's mouth tightened. She gave her head a good shake, sending that ponytail of hers whirling once. "Forget it. You want to piss off Jason that's not my problem."

"You're right. It's not. Just like Jason has no reason to be pissed at me." Jenny grabbed her own bag, not even bothering to slip on her sandals, and walked out of the dugout wearing nothing but her dirt-stained softball socks.

"Screw Jason," she said. "Screw Alice. Screw the whole damn team."

They had no idea what she was dealing with. They had no idea what her life was like. What her father was like. "And I have no intention of telling any of them."

Jenny's plan continued. Every practice, whether with the team or one on one with Chuck, every game, she went through the motions. She did her job. That was all.

She never tried. Never tried hard.

She refused to become the legacy, the future her dad wanted.

Chuck knew. Every time she touched a ball, held a bat, he knew. He said nothing.

If the team knew, or if Coach Steele suspected, they said nothing. Most likely because they were so focused on the upcoming game against Mount Crest. They didn't have time or the energy to look too closely at Jenny, who for all purposes, was still performing. Not even the pimply newspaper reporter asked.

After all Jenny was still playing well, just not as well as she could.

She still played, still started, but her place in the batting lineup slowly moved down. Very slowly. Not noticeable unless you were looking for it.

She was. Chuck was.

So was Jason.

Jenny saw it, every time their eyes met, held, she saw it. He never said anything. He stopped coming by for lunch.

She locked her disappointment, her hurt into the small corner of her soul and refused to think about him.

It was better that way.

That's what she told herself, what she tried to convince her heart every time when he would look away, the disappointment in his face. Every time her chest tightened, hurt. She told herself it didn't matter.

And it didn't.

She wouldn't be in this school long enough for it to matter. In a few short months, when the school year ended Jason will have graduated and she'd be re-packing her boxes and tossing out the ugly floral curtains again.

That's the way her life went.

Jason didn't seem to get it. Or if he did, he wasn't okay with accepting it like Jenny had.

Mount Crest, the big game, crept closer and for the first year in nearly a decade, Sunny View was on their heels. They were only a few games out of winning the Championship, thanks in part to Jenny— even though her performance had dropped.

Coach Steele had pushed the girls at practices all week and this one was no exception. Jenny's breath heaved in and out, the cramp in her side beginning to feel not just annoying but excruciating. When Steele called practice and told everyone to rest up, Jenny was more than grateful.

So was the team. They also didn't hang around in the dugout, didn't chat for the usual twenty minutes when practice ended. Everyone peeled themselves off the dirt, grabbed their stuff, and limped back to the cars to recover.

Jenny lingered. She didn't know why. Maybe she just didn't want to share in her misery, share—as part of the team—her own bumps, bruises, and sore muscles.

She stretched out her legs, untied one cleat, and let it flop down. God, she hurt!

"Jenny."

Jason's voice snatched Jenny up from her quiet peace and solitude. He stood framed in the dugout, the twilight sun stretching behind him making him harder to see. Darker. More imposing.

And more determined than she'd ever seen him.

"Jason."

It was the first time they'd talked, the first time they'd been face to face in weeks. He'd been avoiding her.

Jenny lifted her head. "Is there something you want?"

"Yeah." He didn't move. "I want to know why you're doing this."

She shrugged, letting the motion show that she didn't care—which was completely opposite of her insides, from her thundering heart and her sparking stomach.

She swallowed, tried to calm her nerves. It didn't work.

Then he moved, faster than she'd known he was capable. He knelt before her, close enough she knew he could smell the sweat pouring off her, the ripeness of her knee pads.

He didn't care about the smells, about her sweat. All he cared about was her. It… it wasn't possible.

Jenny's head spun. "What… what are you doing?"

"I'm talking to you. Right now. I know why you're doing this, but I want to hear you say it."

TWENTY-NINE

J enny sat up straighter, putting distance between them, from Jason's kneeling form. It was only inches, but it helped. Every inch helped her breath steady, every heart beat slow, become more even.

It wasn't enough, not nearly enough. Not when Jason was so close. Not when she wanted him closer—even though he stared at her with such intensity, with such… simmering anger.

And yes. He was angry.

"I know what's going on. I know what you're doing."

Yeah, well, she was angry too. "I don't see how that's any of your business."

"It's my business. It's the whole team's business!"

"The hell it is." She shoved him back, tipping him backwards, but he caught himself before he fell onto his ass. "This isn't my team. *They* aren't my team. I play because I don't have a God damn choice, so don't try to throw this crap about being 'part of the team' on me."

"You don't think they deserve to know? That you're out there playing half-hearted while they're giving it everything? They're working their asses off while you're just going through the motions."

Coach Steele may not have noticed Jenny's performance, but Jason sure had. Just like she'd expected. It also didn't help that her stomach twisted, agreeing with him.

The team was working hard.

It wasn't her fault.

Jenny grabbed onto the bench, dug her fingers into the cool metal. It wasn't her fault. "I never asked for this. I never asked to play."

"You may not have asked for it," Jason growled from where he knelt, "but whether you like it or not, you're part of this team and you're *hurting* them."

Jenny shot to her feet.

So did Jason. "That's right, Jenny. Is that hard to hear? You're hurting them, breaking them. What the hell do you think is gonna happen when they find out? When they realize you were *using* them to get back at your dad?"

"I'm not using them!"

She wasn't. She didn't mean to. She had no choice.

"Let's be honest. For once, let's you and me be honest—can you tell me you didn't pick this team just so you could shine? Just so you could look great before you were swept off to another team?"

"I had nothing to do with it." Tears filled her eyes, pricked the corners. "I had no choice."

"Looks to me like you've got a choice now. A choice you're throwing back in their face. After everything they did to welcome you, make you feel like one of them. After everything I did to stick up for you." His voice broke. It was just a moment, but if anything it only fueled Jason's anger. "You used me. You're using them. Just admit it."

"I'm not." She sounded small, weak, lost. She deserved his anger. Welcomed it. But God did it hurt because he was right. He was right about her.

"Then what the hell are you doing?" Jason glared down at her, towering over her.

Just like her father would.

Her father.

The one who'd put her in this position, who'd forced her to take such drastic measures.

"I'm trying to survive!" She shoved him again. Hard. This time he stumbled into the fence.

It surprised both of them. Jason was nearly twice her size.

The surprise didn't last long for Jenny, not when she felt every frustration, every moment of panic, of being alone, of being told what to do, who to be.

This time her tears fell. She didn't fight them. "You think you know anything about me? About my life? You don't. The team doesn't."

Jason pushed away from the fence, but didn't tear his gaze away from her cheeks, from her tears. He made no move to comfort her. "I know what you're going through. I know what your father's pushing you to become. You think you hide it well, but you don't. And this," he gestured to the field, "what you're doing, isn't going to make it go away."

"Oh and you know so well, huh?" She wiped at her eyes, hating herself for crying in front of him, hating him more because she just wanted to hit him, to take all her frustrations out on him just because she *could*. Unlike her dad who she couldn't touch.

Who never cared if she was upset. If she cried.

"Let me guess, you know because you've been there yourself?" Jenny snapped. "You've been the one the big guys were salivating over, the papers writing about you every chance they got, how you'd be the next big pro to come out of Southern California?"

Jason's smile twisted. If you could even call it a smile. "Yeah. Something like that."

"Something like that?" She repeated. "Yeah, you know so much about baseball, about softball, but neither you or anyone else will tell me how. And guess what, Jason, until you can back it up those are empty words just like I've heard my entire life."

He didn't budge. "I know enough to say what you're doing won't work and you need to stop."

He reached for her. Jenny snapped her arm away.

"I don't need to stop anything because I don't have a damn choice. Do you understand now? I *have* to play. I have no choice. None. The only thing I have control over is when I step onto the field. Every pitch, every at bat."

More tears fell, but she didn't stop. Jason was the one who'd pushed this onto her, onto them. She'd give him exactly what he wanted.

"Jason. I'm sixteen. He's already called college teams. He's already arranged for scouts to watch me."

The grim line of Jason's face darkened, became more imposing, more determined. "Jen —"

"No. You listen." She stepped forward, invading his space and not caring. He needed to understand. Even if was only so he didn't hate her quite so much, that it took the tiniest edge out of his anger as watched her, studied her. "I met my first scout when I was ten. Ten. The day I was born he bought a bottle of champagne to celebrate with his team—but the bottle was never opened."

Jason slipped closer. Jenny's heart beat faster, but she wouldn't think of that—not now. She had to say this, had to focus because the second she let herself hesitate, she'd back away, she'd close off.

She didn't know why she wanted to tell him.

"Why wasn't it opened?" he asked.

"Because I wasn't a boy." A tear trickled down her nose. "I wasn't his legacy. So he decided to invest everything—*everything*—into making me a legacy he could have."

"It doesn't have to be this way."

He reached for her. Jenny stepped back.

"Yes. Yes. It does."

"The hell with that." He grabbed her, pulled her against his chest, and kissed her. Kissed her with everything he had, with every emotion Jenny could feel zinging through his skin, through him.

Her whole world narrowed, sparked, and became a raging inferno of electricity. She felt Jason over every inch of her. Felt him in her breath, in her beating heart even as her world spun out of control.

And she didn't want it to stop. Didn't want him to stop holding her, kissing her, caring about her.

Caring. Loving.

Jenny yanked herself free. She trembled, hardly able to stand, but Jason gave her the distance, didn't reach for her like she thought he would. And was grateful when he didn't.

But his eyes sparked with the same intensity she knew were in hers. That want. That need.

"You get it now?" he whispered. "It's my business. You've made this my business and there's no way in hell I'm going to let you throw your life—and your future—away."

"It's…it's not your business. It's my life." Her voice wasn't steady. Far, far from steady. This shouldn't matter. His kissing her shouldn't matter.

So why the hell did it?

Jason touched her bottom lip. His finger brushed her once, then twice. "Yes," he whispered back, just as softly. "It is your life, but now it's mine too."

THIRTY

Jason wasn't a quitter. From what little Jenny knew of him, and if that kiss was any indication, he wasn't about to give up on her. He was focused, determined, and he wouldn't back down just because she'd yelled at him.

Not to mention kissing him right back didn't exactly help her argument that she didn't need help.

Or him.

Jenny groaned and dropped her head onto the biology desk. She hadn't been able to stop thinking about Jason or that stupid kiss.

He'd kissed her, pretty much declared her life was *his* business, and she'd done the only thing she could think of: she'd bolted.

The last thing she needed was Jason distractions. Didn't she have enough problems? The big game getting closer, and her dad was dropping hints about going.

The thought made her stomach curl.

Just last night—right after the kiss—her dad had remembered to call and didn't stop talking about how excited he was to see her play, to pitch.

But he wouldn't be excited. Not when he finally paused in his big baseball season long enough to get a real close look at Jenny's stats.

She was walking a fine line right now and it wouldn't be long before her noticed her performance had slipped....

Jenny touched her still tingling lips. Thoughts of Jason were going to be the least of Jenny's problems.

Alice knocked Jenny from her thoughts when she hit Jenny's chair with her backpack. The chair shifted and Jenny's forehead smacked onto the desk.

"Oh. Sorry." There was nothing sorry in her voice.

Jenny clenched her fists. Breathe. Just breathe. One problem at a time—and let's face it, Alice and her attitude were the least of Jenny's problems. She just needed to keep her cool, keep the team (which included Alice) from looking too closely at her. If they did they might notice what her dad had failed to see.

"It's fine," Jenny said. "I was in the way."

Alice blinked, surprised. Actually, Jenny surprised herself with how calm she sounded, as if she truly didn't care if Alice was again being a complete bitch for no stupid reason.

That of course got Jenny's temper up again, so she yanked her biology textbook out. She buried her nose in the book, no idea where they'd actually left off, didn't care, and kept reading.

"What the hell's your problem?" Alice asked.

Hadn't she just *not* gotten into another fight with Alice? "Nothing. I'm fine."

"Bullshit."

She shrugged. She refused to be drawn into a fight. Not today.

Alice said nothing for several minutes. Then, just before class started, grabbed her bag, said, "Screw this," and left.

Really, Jenny couldn't have hoped for a better reaction.

Not only that, but class zipped by. Before she knew it, the lunch bell rang, but as she picked up her bag, ready to dart out the door and hide where Jason couldn't find her, that's when Dan wheeled into the class. He blocked the way so Jenny, and the few students who hadn't left, were trapped.

No one dared ask Dan to move. No one was that stupid.

Jenny dropped her bag on her desk and leaned against it and

waited. No point carrying around three tons worth of books if you didn't need to.

"Professor Bingley," Dan rolled up to the teacher. "I just wanted to let you know my sister, Alice, wasn't feeling well. She's better, but asked me to get any homework assignments."

Professor Bingley nodded, clearly pleased at Dan's thoughtfulness. Jenny, on the other hand, was reeling.

Alice? His sister? How come no one said anything? Sure she'd seen them together, but she'd thought they were, like, dating... boy couldn't she have been more off.

Seeing the way was clear, Jenny grabbed her bag and dashed for the door but Dan had finished collecting the worksheets. Resigned, she followed after him, hoping he wouldn't notice (because clearly if Alice hated Jenny, then her brother—who clearly hated everybody—would despise her). And that's when Dan glanced behind him and noticed Jenny.

And yes, her guess was right.

He despised her.

"Well, well. If it isn't the new, star, transfer student." He turned his wheelchair around.

Jenny scanned the hallway, didn't see any semi-familiar face who could get her away from Dan and his storm cloud. "Uh, yeah. That's me. The transfer part, not the star part."

She moved around him, but Dan shifted his wheels to block her. The way he moved she wouldn't be surprised if he had lots of practice doing just that.

"You're also Jason's new girl."

Jenny blushed. She hated the way her face betrayed her, like even a guy practically blind could read the emotions on her face. But someone like Dan, someone who seemed to thrive on hurting other people, of making them uncomfortable... it was like a home run batting derby.

He grinned. It wasn't a nice grin. More like an 'I've got you' grin.

"I'm also sure Jason's shown you all the ropes, how the team works, defended you against the other girls. See? I'm right. He has." Dan advanced on her and Jenny backed up to keep him from running over her toes.

"He was just being nice." Nice as in stopping his big sister from pounding Jenny.

"Nice," Dan drawled. "He's good at being nice. He's also good at leaving you high and dry. Being there for you one moment and then the next abandoning you. Leaving you behind to suffer, to deal with *his* mess."

Jenny stopped. Dan nearly collided with her but she didn't back down. She shoved her hands on her hips and glared back at this mean, spiteful man.

"That does *not* sound like the Jason I know. He's been there for me and pushed me to do better—even when I was the one being a bitch to *him*—not the other way around."

Dan's smile curled into a snarl. He smacked her shin with his chair and she stumbled, but quickly regained her balance. She knew his type and she wouldn't give him an inch. Not after everything Jason had done to defend her. Even against his own sister.

"You don't know anything about Jason," he spat. "Or how the only thing he knows how to do is wreck people's careers. He'll do the same to you. Oh, yes, you and your big baseball father. The one mistake you made was befriending Jason."

Dan shot a finger at her chest. She was done listening to him. Finished.

But Dan wasn't.

"How do you think I ended up in this wheelchair? You think I was born this way? Think again."

Jenny's mouth went dry. There was no way—Jason couldn't be responsible. That was… that was impossible!

But Jason never talked about baseball. He never said why he quit; why he'd walked away from the game.

Dan must have seen her hesitation. "He's the one who put me in this wheelchair. He's the reason I can never walk again, can never play baseball again."

"That can't be true."

"It is."

Jenny remembered Alice's reaction to Jason, to baseball. She even remembered the one time she'd overheard Alice and Dan talking in the hallway, how he said he wouldn't go to her game because of Jason.

Because Jason would be there.

True or not, no one had told her. Jason hadn't told her.

She spun around, her backpack thumping against her. She was done being lied to. Done with people keeping secrets from her.

She had enough from her father. She would not stand it from Jason. Not after that kiss. Not after… after the way he made her feel.

She swallowed back a wave of tears. No crying. Not until she talked to Jason and found out what the hell was going on and why he hadn't told her.

But first she had to find him. And there was only one person who'd know where he was.

Lacey.

THIRTY-ONE

As mad as she was, Jenny couldn't stop feeling Jason's kiss. It lingered on her lips, like a whisper, haunting her. Hurting her in a way that Dan never could.

Jason had kissed her, and made her feel alive and wanted… and he hadn't told her. He'd purposefully dodged all her questions, had purposefully kept the truth from her.

Jenny found Lacey where she always was. Eating with the team. A team that also included a now-feeling-better Alice. Jenny shoved thoughts of Alice away. Alice wasn't important. Finding Jason and talking to him was.

But the second Lacey spotted Jenny, she perked up as if ready for a little banter of a fight.

Not this time.

"Where's your brother?"

"In a rush for another kiss are you?"

The girls giggled, but Jenny ignored them. How the hell did she know? Did Jason tell her? Or was it some stupid twin thing?

Jenny clenched the strap of her backpack and fought for calm, found a scrap of it, and barely held on. It wouldn't take much for Lacey to push her, for Jenny to lose it completely.

"Where is he?"

"Baseball field. Helping the freshman kid again." Lacey didn't bother to cover her mouth when she answered. Jenny got the full view of a half-cooked cheeseburger with extra tomatoes and ketchup. "Why? You finally admit he's your boyfriend?"

It was her boyfriend comment that did it.

The same comment Jenny had made to Jason ages ago about not wanting or needing a boyfriend. The same comment that got her into this mess with the dance, a dance she was *not* going to, even if it *was* coming up quickly (all those stupid fliers reminded her like a ticking time bomb). And now, now she knew he'd been keeping things from her.

Big things.

"*If* he was my boyfriend, then I wouldn't have just found out that Dan blames Jason for putting him in a wheelchair and ending his career. In fact, if he *was* my boyfriend, I would have known this little fact a long time ago, along with what the hell happened and why Jason has refused to play baseball ever again."

Silence stretched across the lunch area. Even the baseball team who sat beside the girls, quieted, looked away. They hunched their heads low. No one said anything.

No one denied it either.

For Jenny, it was more than enough confirmation. No, Jason hadn't lied to her, but he'd omitted the truth—which in her book, was just as bad.

Alice clutched a Coke can until it crinkled under her grip. Her face had turned a ghostly white. She wouldn't meet Jenny's gaze.

So. It was true.

They all blamed Jason.

"Jenny…." Elizabeth slowly stood from her seat, warning her.

Lacey huffed a very deliberate breath. She swallowed her burger, wiped her mouth, but missed the mustard stain. She stood—no—she towered over Jenny.

"You better be very careful what you say, Transfer."

"Why?" Jenny crossed her arms. No more running away. No more pretending. "How am I supposed to know, Lacey? After all, this team *grew up* together. How is the new girl supposed to know what she should and shouldn't say? What subjects have you decided are off-limits? Especially when those subjects are about the guy you keep saying I'm dating."

Who she wasn't dating. Not now. Not ever.

For a moment, Lacey turned into the Giant she first met. All arms, all anger, all protecting of this team. And of her brother, apparently. The brother who'd always protected Jenny.

But Lacey didn't have a chance to answer.

Alice answered for her.

"They don't talk about it because of me." Alice glared at Jenny with a cool, sharp anger—a complete contrast to Lacey's fiery one. "Because it was Jason's fault my brother lost his shot at the Majors. Because Jason was driving when they got into the accident. Because while Jason decided not to play anymore, my brother *can't*. Ever again. There, Little Miss Princess, are you happy now? Is the team's full disclosure satisfied, because if it is I'd like to hear from you."

Jenny didn't like the sound of that, but she wouldn't back down. "What about me?"

"Why don't we start with you and last game? How you *should* have beaten the throw to third but you didn't." Alice jumped to her feet, ponytail nearly smacking Elizabeth in the face. "Or how about letting Fitzgerald get the winning hit. You *should* have had her. You had the count loaded. You had her set up perfectly and yet *she* smacked a line drive off you. A hit that won the game."

One by one, the team slowly turned to Jenny, a question in their eyes, written as black as night on their faces. They wanted an answer.

She had none to give them.

Jenny stood there, back straight, head tall.

Alice snorted. "Well, I guess the full disclosure only applies to us." She slammed back into her seat, eyes locked on the table. Hurt. Pissed.

Not even Elizabeth tried to defend Jenny. In fact, she wouldn't even look at her. Elizabeth knew. She, out of everyone, would have seen

Jenny's performance decline. And she, out of everyone, would have known the reason why.

Jenny didn't feel any anger from Elizabeth, unlike the rest of the team. But still, Jenny deserved it.

Elizabeth, who'd stayed silent during the whole exchange, scooted closer to Alice. Alice yanked away, but Elizabeth didn't move. She didn't try to touch or comfort Alice. But she was there, if Alice needed it.

The rest of the team followed suit. Some drifted closer, others stayed where they were, but there was no denying the protective posture, the narrowed way they watched Jenny.

Daring her to say anything else.

Jason had been right. She was hurting the team.

But hadn't she known this was going to happen? Hadn't she'd known she'd steal their smiles? She had. It just wasn't the reason she thought it would be. Instead of the cause being her father or his money or his legacy, this time it had been Jenny.

This time it was all on Jenny and her selfish attitude.

Lacey threw her crumpled, stained burger wrapper in the trashcan. It missed. "I think you should leave."

"Yeah. I think you're right."

Jenny turned, and left. She knew, in her heart, she'd never be back. Not to lunch. Not to *Joe's* for some pizza with Lacey and Elizabeth. She would never allow herself to sit with them again, not after today, not after what she'd done.

What she—and she alone—had been the cause of.

The team's hurt would grow, would worsen when they realized Alice was right, that their chances of winning the Championship fell every time Jenny stepped onto the field.

They'd hate her even more.

She'd deserve it.

But that didn't mean she could back out now. Not when she had no other choice. There was no other way.

Tears pricked the corners of her eyes and she wiped them away as she dodged the bodies of students, as she ignored the questioning looks from the baseball team.

She'd cry later, but first she had to talk with Jason. She'd end things with him, just like she'd done with the team, and then… and then she'd deal with her father.

Somehow, she'd deal with him too.

After all, it wasn't like her heart could break any further, not after today.

THIRTY-TWO

Other than Blake, the freshman pitcher, Jason was alone. He sat behind the plate, baseball hat turned backwards, glove outstretched as Blake threw another pitch. A strike, smacking the inside corner of the plate. The impact sent a cloud of dust from Jason's glove.

He said something to Blake, and while Jenny was too far to hear, she could easily see his smile.

Her stomach twisted at the sight.

Smiling and happy. He wouldn't feel that way when she was finished, when she'd said what she needed to say.

Jenny didn't give herself a chance to think. If she did she might back out, might lose her nerves and fall into the same easy lies her mom did with her dad.

He'd meant to tell her, but it slipped his mind.

It was for the best. She shouldn't worry about it and just trust him.

Or, Jenny's favorite, he didn't want to worry her.

The hell with that. She wanted to worry. She wanted to know about Jason's life, the good and the bad. But more than anything she deserved to know the truth.

Jenny dropped her backpack onto the bleachers, sending a loud

CLANK across the field, announcing her presence. Jason's eyes lit up when he saw her, the same way he'd looked at her the night before, seconds before he kissed her.

But then he noticed her long, determined strides. The way her arms swung back and forth at her side, fists clenched.

Both Jason and Blake took one look at her and knew something was up. In Blake's case, he thanked Jason for helping out and took off.

Smart boy.

Jason slowly rose from his crouched position over home plate and turned his baseball hat forward. "Jenny."

"Were you ever going to tell me? Were you ever going to tell me the *reason* you quit baseball? Or were you just going to keep pushing me away and keep that little tidbit to yourself?"

The wariness in Jason's posture shifted, tensed. Good. She didn't want an apology. She wanted answers. She wanted the truth.

"Baseball," he said, "and why I walked away from it is my business."

She grabbed his glove and waved it in his face. The ball rolled free. Fell to the ground. "Your business? And what about me?"

"It has nothing to do with you unless I knew you a year ago and you forgot to mention it."

"Oh, so you can butt your nose into my damn business, but you don't *need* tell me yours? That yesterday you were all in my face about softball, about my life—and here you are, telling me to have fun, to keep my head up when you can't even tell me the truth about yourself!"

She threw the glove at his chest. He caught it, but not before another dust cloud spewed into the air, swirled around them.

He dropped the glove. "Are you gonna tell me what this is about or should I just guess?"

"Dan. This is about Dan. Did you know I ran into him? Did you know that he holds *you* responsible for his accident, for being unable to play baseball again? Oh, wait, you must know because both the softball and baseball teams know. Everyone knows. Except me."

Jason's face reddened. So. He knew. He knew exactly what she was talking about, and more importantly, he believed it too. He believed what Dan said.

"It's true." The words whooshed out of her. "And you weren't going to tell me."

"It's not something I'm proud of."

She backed up a step, needing distance between them, needing to breathe, to think. "So that's it then. You're only going to tell me what you're proud of and the rest—what? You're just going to keep to yourself?"

Just like her father.

But unlike her mother, Jenny wasn't going to accept it. Not from Jason. Not when this whole time she thought he'd cared… had actually cared about *her* and not that she was Sam Taylor's daughter.

"It's not like that," Jason said as if he knew exactly what she was thinking. But still, he didn't try to explain. Didn't try to help her understand.

She inched back another step. Then another. "I think it is. You don't want to tell me. You had no intention of telling me anything—and, and I just can't accept that."

She couldn't be with someone who *could* accept that.

The tears from earlier, the ones she'd fought to keep down after the team's rejection, came back. This time, no amount of swallowing or holding her breath would stop them.

Or maybe, it was just because this was Jason and for whatever reason, Jason made her hurt… made her hurt more than the softball team ever could, more than her dad ever could. Like someone was tearing a hole from the inside out.

She pressed a hand against her chest, held it there, and distantly wondered why it was hard to breathe. And it was. It was because she cared about Jason.

No. This was more.

She loved him.

Tears spilled down her face, slid down her cheeks. She loved him and he couldn't tell her the truth.

The thought made her stagger, made her want to hurl.

"Jenny —" Jason lifted his hand as if to reach for her.

"Don't," she whispered. "Oh, God, please don't touch me."

Not now. Not until she made this feeling go away, made it disappear. It wasn't fair! How could she fall in love with him and this whole time he'd kept the truth from her?

Irony. Cruel, God damn irony. That's what this was.

"I don't know what happened with the accident." Her words muffled together, but she wiped at her eyes, knowing she needed to say this, needed to end this right now. "I don't believe there were drugs or alcohol involved. Not with you."

His lips pinched together. He shook his head. Once.

She was right. Then it meant it was just that—an accident. An accident that hadn't been Jason's fault. "You blame yourself. It wasn't your fault, but you blame yourself."

"You weren't there."

"Yeah, and you were and you still blame yourself even though it wasn't your fault. I can see it in your face, Jason. You can lie to me all you want, but your face doesn't lie. Not to me."

It was a talent she'd learned because of her dad. No matter what he said she could always read the truth in his face.

"But I guess this is easier, huh?" she asked. "Easier to let a selfish, miserable boy blame you rather than be thankful for what he does have —that he's alive. And it's easier for you just to accept that blame than realize you made a mistake and to forgive yourself."

Jason flinched at the world 'forgive.' "Dan would never have been on that road, in that car, if it wasn't for me. If I hadn't made a late stop at McDonald's, we wouldn't have been on that road at that exact moment. If I had been paying more attention, I'd have seen the other car. I'd have done something. Reacted. It *is* my fault."

"You're not a superhero!" Jenny shot back. "You're not perfect. You make mistakes. You're human, but that doesn't mean you can blame yourself for the rest of your life. That you should take away your future and your chances just to make Dan feel better."

"I blame myself because it's my fault!" Jason kicked the baseball, hurled it off across the dirt until it bounced off the fence. He rounded on her. "And what about you and you not being honest with you? Your 'plan' to get kicked off the team because you can't stand up to your dad? Because you're afraid he'll never change, will never listen to you?"

For whatever reason, Jason knew her—or maybe it was just because they were so much alike.

Both lost. Both alone.

"I don't have a choice."

"There's always a choice. And maybe, for once, you should actually admit that you chose wrong. That instead of turning your back on your team, you should have told your dad 'no. '"

"The difference," Jenny whispered, "is I don't love softball. Not the way you love baseball. And you still do. Not a day goes by where you don't think about being back on that mound, about stepping up to the plate and hitting the winning run. But not me. I don't *want* to play anymore."

Jason looked away. He shoved his hands into his jean pockets and refused to meet her gaze.

That was fine. That made what she had to say next easier. Even if she hadn't realized what needed to be said until this moment.

Until she saw him standing there, anger and disappointment spiraling off him, looking so much like herself.

"I don't love softball. Not anymore. It's done. Over. And…." She took a deep breath. She needed to say this. For both of them. "And I love you. I love you and I can't."

Jason's head jerked towards her, eyes wide. "Jenny."

"I already have one person in my life I can't trust. I can't love someone who won't tell me the truth, who keeps things from me. You need to find another date to the dance, Jason. I can't go with you. Not ever."

THIRTY-THREE

That afternoon, Jenny snuck out of class early, hoping to meet with Coach Steele before practice. She clutched the letter in her hand, heard the paper crinkle until she loosened her grip.

She had wanted just to drop the letter off and run, run far and fast until this whole place was behind her. But she couldn't. Regardless of what happened, she'd see this through to the end.

She'd give Coach Steele her resignation in person.

The empty halls gave her a quiet strength, encouraged her to walk faster, to hit the outside doors before the bell rang. The whole school, the very air itself, seemed charged to push her, telling her to leave its walls and never come back.

She picked up her pace, reached the softball field just as the bell chimed across campus, and sure enough there was Coach Steele hauling out the gear and bags just like she did every day before practice.

Coach Steele dusted her hands on her already dusty shorts and glanced up when Jenny's shoes shuffled the dirt. "Jenny. You're here early, but why aren't you dressed?"

"I, I'm not...." The words froze in her throat. She couldn't believe she was doing this. Her father, her mother… they were going to kill her when they found out.

But the words wouldn't come. They clogged in her throat, stuck in her mouth.

She'd show Jason he was wrong about her. She was afraid.

Jenny shot her hand out, holding the letter to Coach Steele, and ignored the way both her hand and the letter trembled.

"What's this…." The question in Coach Steele's face vanished as she read. "Jenny. What's this about?"

"Everything and I just, I just can't -" She couldn't do this anymore. Not anymore. She couldn't be her dad's legacy. "I just can't play anymore."

Coach Steele sighed and tucked the letter in her back pocket.

In the distance, Jenny saw the team approaching. It was like they were a single formation, a defensive line protecting each other, keeping back anyone who would threaten the team.

"Let's talk about this after practice?"

"I —"

"I don't know what this is all about, probably team drama or even drama at home. But once you get out there and throw the ball around you'll feel better."

This wasn't what Jenny wanted. Throwing the ball around wouldn't help, wouldn't make her decision any different. Wouldn't make the hurt in her chest go away. Nothing could. Nothing but her dad giving up baseball and settling in one place and calling it a home.

But she had no control over that.

The only thing she had control over was softball and her decision to play—but Coach Steele wasn't listening to her.

"It's not going to change my mind."

"Regardless, now's not the time to talk." Coach Steele wrapped an arm around Jenny's shoulders. It was meant to be comforting. It wasn't.

"The girls are almost here," Steele said. "Just get through practice, do what you can, and then we'll talk. I just can't stand by and let someone of your talent, your skills walk away. I just can't. Not to mention your dad —"

Jenny jerked away. "What about my dad?"

"You know he's not going to take this lightly. That's all I'm saying."

"It's not his choice. It's mine."

But Coach Steele simply nodded and smiled, trying to placate Jenny, but Jenny knew better. And she knew the coach would never accept her resignation, would never let her walk away.

She wanted to cry. To scream. Maybe both. But there was nothing she could do, just go and change like Coach Steele suggested.

Her arms and body moved, wooden and slow. The team filled into the bleachers. They completely ignored her. Everyone except Elizabeth, who watched her with knowing eyes but said nothing.

She was probably outvoted. Probably told by the whole team to leave Jenny alone. To keep her as the outsider she was.

Jason wasn't in the stands.

Jenny was glad.

Even when she changed and came back, Jason was still missing. But Chuck was there, silent, sturdy Chuck. Just seeing him made her want to cry. He was the only one who had her back, the only one who understood and was willing to stand beside her.

Jenny jogged onto the field and joined the warm up session. Or tried to anyway. None of the girls would let her join. It wasn't until Coach Steele ordered Lacey and Elizabeth to throw with Jenny that a ball actually came her way.

No one talked. No one except Elizabeth who mumbled that her doctor had given her the clear to pitch at the big game. This brought smiles to everyone's faces.

Smiles that vanished when they all heard the unmistakable, expensive roar of a sports car tearing into the parking lot. Jenny froze. Her heart kicked into over drive as she spotted the familiar black car and her dad's familiar stance as he stormed out the door and slammed it behind him.

"I thought the Chargers were away this weekend," Elizabeth said to no one in particular, though the question was clearly directed at Jenny.

"They are."

They were. That was where her dad was supposed to be. Except he wasn't in Cleveland. He was here.

At her practice.

And he was furious.

THIRTY-FOUR

She knew what this was about.

Jenny steeled her shoulders, took a deep breath, and went to meet her dad. She walked straight through the two rows of girls who had all stopped warming up to stare.

To stare at her father.

To stare at Jenny.

Her dad stormed towards the field, arms swinging at his side. She heard his stomps vibrating through the earth. It didn't matter if he wore the most expensive pants, recently shined shoes, and a blue silk shirt; even in all that finery there was no mistaking his fury.

Fury at Jenny.

Jenny passed by Coach Steele without a word. She didn't even pause when the coach reached for her.

Jenny simply kept going.

They'd all wanted the truth. Well, it looked like they were going to get it. But instead of meeting Jenny on the softball field, her dad swerved towards the stands.

Towards Chuck.

"Oh, no."

Elizabeth, who had jogged up behind Jenny without her realizing it, reached her side. "What is it? Jenny, what's going on?"

"He's blaming Chuck."

It was wrong. It wasn't Chuck's fault. It was hers!

Chuck stood up from his seat in the stands, looking like the normal guy who just enjoyed watching softball games, the complete opposite of her dad in his red, flannel shirt and faded jeans.

This time there was no shaking of hands, no simple hellos or pleasantries. Just her dad, cocking back his fists, and swinging it at Chuck's face.

"You son of a bitch."

"Dad!" Jenny sprinted forward, Elizabeth at her side.

Behind her, Jenny heard the team move but all her attention was on her Chuck as he neatly ducked his head. He moved in time to miss the brunt of it, but not fast enough. He staggered back as her dad's fist clipped his chin.

Blood cracked on Chuck's bottom lip. Jenny ran faster. Her dad reared up his arm again.

Jenny jumped. She clutched his arm and dug her feet into the ground. "Dad. Stop!"

"Let me go, Jennifer! I'm teaching this God damn scumbag a lesson."

"No!" She dug her feet in harder, pushing back with everything ounce of strength she had. "Please! It's not his fault."

Elizabeth was there, wrapping her hands around Jenny's. Helping her. "Mr. Taylor. Stop!"

He didn't hear them. All his attention was on Chuck.

Jenny hadn't heard her mother approach, hadn't known she'd come with her dad. But her voice whipped through the air, clear, sharp. It cut through the haze surrounding her dad. "Sam. Your hand."

Her father froze. He'd pulled his arm back for another strike, but he didn't finish the swing.

"That's right, your very expensive, important hand that could easily break if you didn't break something already." Her mother moved through the girls—no, they parted for her. All Jenny glimpsed was her tall, immaculate form and the flash of diamonds.

Her mother was here too. Here to see Jenny's humiliation as she hurt the people she cared about most.

Her dad slowly lowered his arm, but his gaze was still locked on Chuck who hadn't moved.

"Good to see you too, Sam." Chuck turned and spit. Drops of blood sprinkled the dirt.

"Screw you, Chuck."

Jenny still clung to her dad's arm, fear holding her there; and she would have kept clinging if her mom hadn't gently extracted first Elizabeth's and then Jenny's hands.

"That's enough, Sam," her mother said. "Coach Steele, I'm terribly sorry we interrupted your practice with this family problem."

Steele mumbled a reply, but Jenny's ears pounded with blood, with adrenaline. She didn't realize she was holding onto Elizabeth until she glanced down and saw the other girl's hands turning white. Jenny immediately released her and backed up a step.

She didn't need help. She didn't need friends. This was her problem, her mess. She'd face her dad and accept the punishment.

"Family problem," her dad repeated. "Yes. Forgive us. This is a family problem." But then he rounded on Chuck and Jenny tensed, ready to jump back in. "What the hell were you thinking? Did you think I wouldn't notice? Wouldn't realize the truth?"

Sweat trickled down Jenny's back, making her practice uniform stick to her. Her mother locked her arms around Jenny, hiding her shivers from her dad, from the team.

"Dad —"

"Quiet, Jennifer."

"But it's not fair," she whispered back even as tears blurred her vision. "This is my fault. Not Chuck's."

"Chuck knew what he was doing."

But he didn't. He couldn't have.

She strained forward but her mom held her in place, held her with a strength Jenny had no idea she had.

"Can't say I know what you're talkin' about, Sam," Chuck replied, just as calm and ordinary as ever.

"Jennifer's performance. Hell, all I had to do was open the damn newspaper," which he ripped out from his back pocket.

Jenny glimpsed the *Sunny View Gazette* and her world narrowed to a pinpoint. An article? About her?

"Samantha Dawson seems to be covering the games and not only that," he spat, "concludes that '*Sam Taylor's legacy might not hold true as his daughter, Jennifer Taylor's, performance on the Sunny View Tigers continues to decline. While the once starter isn't available for comment, it has been noted the coach has dropped her from batting second to fifth. Not only has her hitting performance weakened, her pitching statistics have plummeted right alongside her bat.*"

He threw the paper at Chuck.

Jenny stared at the paper, now laying at Chuck's feet, in shock. Double-D had noticed. She'd never tried to speak with her for a comment since that time in the Chargers clubhouse, but... she'd still put two and two together.

The team, who now surrounded Jenny and her family, seemed to close in. Their eyes were on her and even with her mother there, holding her, Jenny felt exposed. Vulnerable.

Just like she deserved to be.

Jenny lifted her head and met each girl's gaze. Locked eyes with them, told them the truth when words couldn't. They knew. They now all knew the truth.

Alice was the last. But for once there was no satisfaction in Alice's gaze, no triumph of finally having been right.

"Full disclosure," Jenny whispered.

The truth. Just as she had demanded it of the team and then of Jason. Now they had the truth from her.

"This," her dad growled, "is your fault. What the hell do I pay you for? You were *supposed* to make sure she wasn't screwing this up! And the next thing I know this, this crap hits the papers. Do you have any damn idea what I have on the line right now? For her future?"

"Yes, sir," Chuck replied, "I do. I know about the deals. I know about the big schools who've marked Jenny's senior year on their calendar. About the deals with Louisville and Nike."

Coach Steele's head jerked towards Chuck. "What? Schools? Nike?"

But Chuck kept going. "And I know it's easy to blame me. I *am* the guy you pay to keep her in top shape, but frankly, Boss. You can go screw yourself."

Her mother gasped, dropping her hold of Jenny to cover her mouth. "Chuck!"

"And frankly," Chuck steamrolled over both her mom and dad's sudden inhale, "the only person you have to blame is yourself, Sam. She's a good kid. She works hard, but the hell with your plans. This is her life and her future. If you want her to play her best, maybe you should include her on those plans once in a while."

Jenny's face heated as everyone's eyes went to her. Shock. Surprise.

It was all there.

Everyone except her dad who even now refused to look at her, refused to acknowledge what was right in front of him.

"Dad," she whispered. "It's not Chuck's fault. It's mine."

"The only person who's at fault, Jennifer, is Chuck."

More tears fell. "Why won't you listen?"

"Chuck. You're fired."

"Dad!" Jenny jerked forward, but it was Elizabeth who caught her, then Lacey. They held her back even as she struggled to get forward to make him see, make him understand.

"He won't listen," Elizabeth said under her breath. "Jenny, just let it go."

"No. Not when it's not his fault. It's mine."

Lacey's hands tightened. "You're not the one to blame."

But she was. This was all her fault. Everything. From taking this wonderful team and turning it into this, for getting Chuck fired.

Jenny had no one to blame but herself.

Chuck nodded, then swept off his Chargers cap and threw it at her dad. "I have no problems with that. Probably should have resigned years ago when you stole her smile. But then, I thought you were right. I thought you were right about her future. But now? Now I know you're nothin' but another selfish, big-time player."

Her dad stepped forward. Her mom was there, placed a calming hand on his chest. "Enough, Sam, just let it go."

"Jenny, however," Chuck said, "Jenny deserves a hell of a lot more than you've given her. Not your big-time sponsors or chances of a big future, but a life. A life with friends, a life with that boy who makes her smile brighter than I've ever seen her."

Jenny stiffened as her dad finally looked at her, his eyes piercing her where she was between Elizabeth and Lacey.

"She deserves," Chuck pushed on, uncaring of the spot he suddenly put her in, "to be happy. The life you've given her? That's the furthest thing from happiness, and I feel sorry for her. And for you."

Her dad puffed out a breath, then another. Jenny thought for sure he was going to tackle Chuck, but her mom held her place there, fingers splayed on that now wrinkled silk shirt.

"Jennifer." He nodded once to Jenny. "I'm sorry I've let you down. Truly."

He left. He said nothing else, just quietly slipped away. His feet padded on the soft dirt, then the cement path as he headed up the walkway to the parking lot.

No one said anything, they all just watched his departing form.

Her dad crushed the Chargers hat in his hand and threw it in the trashcan. "Carol. I'm late for my flight. Get that girl in shape by the Mount Crest game. I don't care what you do...." His furious blue eyes knifed through Jenny. "But get rid of that boy or both you and Jenny will lose those privileges you enjoy off my salary."

Her mom paled and after a slight hesitation, nodded. "Yes, Sam. Of course."

She watched him leave and the second his back was turned, she pulled Jenny to her and kissed her forehead. It was a kiss Jenny couldn't feel. Her body was numb, her heart was solid, frozen.

This was all her fault.

"Don't you worry. A boy who cares about you that much is worth a thousand of the diamonds your father gives me." She kissed Jenny's forehead again as if she needed to prove her point, as if she needed to feel that Jenny was still solid, still real within her arms.

"His name's Jason." Jenny was surprised to hear her own voice, though it was hoarse as if she hadn't used it in years. "And he's just a friend."

A friend who now hated her. Just like everyone else.

In the end, they needed a ride home and it was Laurie who seemed to be there right when her mom was about to collapse, who offered to drive.

"No point staying for practice." Laurie tucked Jenny into the seat and buckled her up. "And you know, Carol, you're not alone in this. You never were."

Her mom gave Laurie a weak smile. "Thank you, but I'm a little too old to start learning my lesson. Sam's a good man, but he's just so focused on his own life. It's not his fault."

"Maybe." Laurie closed Jenny's door and slid into the driver's seat. "But you're never too old for a friend. And I think you need one right now."

Jenny closed her eyes and let their silence drift over her.

Friends. She had none. And after today, she didn't deserve any.

It was good the Mount Crest game was coming soon. One way or another, this would all be over.

THIRTY-FIVE

Jenny had hoped she'd have the weekend to herself. Just her and her mom. In the end, she wasn't so lucky. Her dad flew to Cleveland, as planned, played the first of three games, but was then on the first plane back to Sunny View. When Jenny trudged down the stairs, eyes red and swollen from her sleepless night, he was waiting for her at the kitchen table.

The paper was there also, waiting for her.

"I couldn't trust your mom to do this right, not when it's your future at stake. Read it." He slammed his hand on top. "Read it until you have every word memorized and then get your glove. We're going to practice."

Jenny stood there, hand frozen on the kitchen counter. All she could do was nod.

He'd make her practice. Make her go and go and go until she fell.

Fine. But she wouldn't' give an inch. No matter what he said, no matter what he did, she was done with softball. Done with him controlling her life and if he refused to listen, like now as he scraped the chair back and stalked into the living room… the hell with him.

She *was* taking control of her life.

And if the only way she could get that across to him was at the Mount Crest game, then so be it.

Brutal.

It was the only word that described her weekend. A relentless, never-ending nightmare of pitching, hitting in the backyard batting cage, and even more pitching. The worst part wasn't her dad drilling her, it was Jason. Jason who kept calling all weekend. Tried her cell, her home phone (thank God her mom always answered the phone), even her email. She hadn't answered, hadn't returned one call. She couldn't—didn't dare face him.

Because he'd been right about her. This whole time, he'd been right.

She was too afraid to stand up to her dad.

By the time Monday came around Jenny could barely walk. Every muscle hurt, every step made her groan, but every time she thought of Jason the ache in her heart was worse. Much worse.

Her mother took one look at her, pressed her lips into a tight line, and said, "I'm calling you in sick."

"But mom, I can't —"

"Oh, yes you can. If your father can work you into the ground all weekend, then I can call in sick and take you to the spa for a nice message and hope to hell you get enough feeling into your limbs to play tomorrow."

Tomorrow. The big game.

Jenny stifled a shudder. She hoped Coach Steele had changed her mind about letting her play, about having her as relief pitcher for Lacey. But when her mom made the call—both to the school and to Coach Steele—she was told it wouldn't a problem.

"Coach Steele said you're starting second base tomorrow. She wants to you to rest up and relax. I think we can handle that, don't you?"

Jenny didn't think so. Not when all she wanted was to throw up.

There went her last chance of backing out. Coach Steele was going to make her play… which meant she had to go through with this. Even if it might cost the team the game, cost them the league championship… Jenny squeezed her eyes closed.

She had no choice.

Like anything in high school, word travels fast. When the news was about the fight between Jenny and her famous father, word traveled faster than light speed.

What did surprise her was that on Tuesday everyone kept their distance. Sure they looked at her, watched as if they *knew* what had happened, but no one said anything. No one tried to take advantage of the situation, tried to be her new 'best friend.'

Jenny slipped her books for first period into her bag. It seemed like a lifetime ago since she'd been down these halls, since she'd talked with Dan and confronted Jason. And the last time she smiled? God, she couldn't even remember what day it had been, like a memory already half faded and forgotten.

"Probably because it was." She closed her locker and clicked the lock shut. It was better this way. Better for her to have distance. Easier for the team to hate her when it was all finished.

Lacey slammed her hand against the locker nearest to Jenny's. "I was wondering if you'd ever show your face again."

Jenny jerked back in surprise, then relaxed when she saw it was Lacey. "Me too."

Lacey, with her white muscle shirt and softball hat, looked even more intimidating than when Jenny had first met her. Or it could just be because she looked like she wanted to throttle someone.

Probably Jenny.

"That's it? Me too? Are you already to lie down and let him win?"

Jenny blinked. "What? What are you —?"

"Quit stuttering and try to keep up." Lacey grabbed Jenny's arm and yanked her down the hall. "You and I need to talk."

Lacey didn't stop pulling until they were outside… well outside and away from the rest of the student body, Jenny noted. As in, they were standing in the center of the softball infield, both girls with their backpacks and watching the morning clouds slowly dissolve away as the sun's light streaked through.

"There. This looks about good." Lacey released Jenny who staggered a few safe feet away.

"Good for what? To kill me?"

"Nah. I don't want to kill you. Unless of course, you decide to be a bitch about this whole thing with my brother. Then I'd kill you."

"Jason?" Jenny's breath caught in her throat. She'd so badly wanted to talk with him—but she couldn't. "It's better this way."

"The hell it is." Lacey thumped a hand into Jenny's chest, and she staggered back another step. "What would be better is if you stood up for yourself instead of letting people like me, people like your asshole of a dad, jerk you around. Personally, I don't give a shit. But my brother does and apparently, so do you."

Jenny's mouth worked. Nothing came out.

Lacey leaned in, the brim of her hat poking Jenny in the forehead. "That's what I thought. You are in love with him."

Her face heated. "No! Of course not."

"Bullshit."

Lacey gave her the kind of look that dared Jenny to argue with her. Jenny clicked her mouth shut. Arguing was stupid—especially when Lacey was actually right. For a change.

"So. You like him. You love him."

Jenny swallowed. Nodded.

"Good. Then that means this thing going on, this thing between you, me, the team, it means we're going to talk and work it out."

Now Jenny was really confused. "Work it out? Lacey, you know what I've been doing all season. You know I haven't —"

"Does it look like I give a shit?"

In that case…."No."

"Good. That means we understand each other, so listen up because I'm only going to say this once. That idiot is madly in love with you, and nothing I've said is getting through his thick head."

Actually, it was Jenny's head that was spinning like mad. "In love? With me?"

Lacey snorted. "Yeah, that's what I said."

He hadn't said anything. When she told him she loved him… he hadn't said anything. Jenny rocked back on her heels. Her backpack slipped free from her shoulders, but Lacey reached out and easily caught it.

"Shocking, isn't it? But not so shocking as the idea of what happens next. You're going to play, to start against Mount Crest like we'd planned. Elizabeth is cleared to pitch but she's gonna step aside and let you."

"No! She can't. I'll —"

Lacey grabbed Jenny's shoulder with her meaty paw. "We know what you're going to do, and I'm telling you now, you do what you have to do."

Jenny's mouth went dry. Lacey… Lacey couldn't be saying what Jenny thought she was saying.

"You do what you need to on the field," Lacey said, "but you will go to that dance with Jason. Just like you promised."

She hadn't promised anything. "I—I mean… is he going to play baseball? Is he going to play again?"

Lacey tilted her head, curious. "Funny you should ask that. He had his bat out yesterday. The first time in a year he's taken it out. But I don't know. You gonna get all pretty and dressed up?"

"I," she took a deep breath. "I don't know."

"Then me neither. I guess it's up to him to decide. And you." Lacey patted Jenny's shoulder and offered a small smile. It was small, tiny even, but it was actually a smile.

Jenny had never seen Lacey smile before.

"Whatever happens out there, no hard feelings. We're your team. We'll pick up the slack. And that dance, you know? It's not actually just any ol' dance."

"It's—it's not." Jenny was having a hard time thinking, let alone speaking. Lacey was encouraging to her? She was being *nice?*

"It's the senior prom."

THIRTY-SIX

While Lacey being nice was… shocking, Jenny found if she took a few deep breaths her vision evened itself out and she didn't pass out from shock on the field. But it was that last bit about Jason, about the dance being the *senior prom*, now *that* nearly knocked her down.

Thankfully, Lacey had managed to finish off with all the enlightening and shocking bits of the conversation at that point, and then manhandled/hauled Jenny all the way to homeroom before the bell rang.

"There you go. Right back as promised." Lacey dropped her off outside her classroom.

Jenny straightened her Tigers hat, still reeling from the conversation, when her gaze slid across Jason's homeroom. She could see him inside, shoulders hunched forward, head lowered.

Even from here she felt his sadness, his misery. It touched her, right to that stupid spark in her stomach and she felt something open and tear at the sight.

He'd always been so happy, so relaxed and inviting. Now look what she'd done—what she'd done to him.

He glanced up, as if feeling her gaze on him. Their eyes meant. His widened. He half rose from his seat, ready to tear across the small space separating them.

Jenny's heart thundered and she yearned to be in his arms again, to feel his kiss, his strength.

Then she remembered her father's words when she left for school this morning and her body tensed.

Don't fail me. Don't let that boy distract you.

He'd said he'd know if Jason distracted her, if she lost her focus on the game because of him. She had no intention of bringing Jason into her mess, especially if he did decide to play baseball again. Her father was a very bad enemy to have.

Jason felt the shift in her and stopped, half out of his seat, a question in his eyes. She dropped her gaze and shook her head. She couldn't do this. She couldn't be with him.

And after today, it wouldn't matter.

Her dad would pull her from the team, from Sunny View, but at least she'd have won. She'd have shown him just how far she'd go.

The bell rang and the moment between her and Jason was broken.

Thank God. Because she knew, even as she settled into the safety of her seat, she would break in Jason's arms. The second she felt his protection, his warm embrace, all her plans, everything, would fall apart.

She wouldn't carry her plan through.

And she had to.

She simply had to.

Alice who came in a few minutes after Jenny didn't talk to her. She scowled once, like always, but this time the look was deeper, sharper. As if she really did hate Jenny with her entire being.

And Jenny deserved it. She'd stolen Alice's spot on the team and was purposefully throwing it aside.

Jenny didn't blame her one bit.

Dan, however, had no problems blaming Jenny. He was waiting for her at the end of biology, rocking back and forth on his chair, giving her that twisted smile of his.

"Well, well. If it isn't the superstar whose dad fired her personal coach."

Jenny hefted her backpack higher on her shoulder. "Leave me alone, Dan. I'm not in the mood."

"Not in the mood?" He wheeled in front of her, cutting off her escape route. "Gee. That's too bad. What are you in the mood for? Ruining my sister's chances at a big future? A big scholarship she might steal from you?"

Jenny's hands tightened. She moved again, but Dan was there.

"Poor, poor, Jenny. Jenny with everything in the world except friends, except a home, and now no more Jason."

Her back straightened. A home. She didn't have a home, didn't know what a home felt like and never would again. But that didn't mean she'd let a spineless, selfish ass throw it in her face.

"You know what?" she snapped. "Please, feel sorry for me. If that makes you feel better, if taunting me and making me feel like crap helps you get through your day, then have at it." She stepped forward, for once forcing Dan to wheel back a step. "But the person I'm really sorry for is you. You who can't smile, who can't do anything but taunt me and scowl. All you do is carry your big stupid cloud around because you can't play baseball. Well, guess what? There's more to life than baseball."

Dan's mouth clicked open.

Jenny pushed on, feeling all her frustration spill out. "And if you had your head out of your ass long enough you'd realize you were alive and you still had an amazing friend because Jason hasn't forgiven himself for what happened. He'll never play again because that makes *you* feel better. So go screw yourself, Dan, but I'm not going to feel sorry for you. Not anymore!"

Jenny stormed off—stormed right through the crowd who'd gathered behind her. Including Alice, who stared at Jenny with a mix of shock and hatred.

So what else was new?

But Lacey was right.

Jenny needed to stand up for herself and if she had to start first with Dan… then it was a start because right now she had a game to focus on.

A game which she still didn't know if she should try her best or try her worst.

THIRTY-SEVEN

Every parking spot was filled. Every spare seat in the bleachers was taken. It was the big Sunny View vs. Mount Crest game, but it was more than that. The whole school had shown up to see how Jenny Taylor, the daughter of famous baseball player, Sam Taylor, would play. To see if she'd excel like her father or if she'd choke and lose it all.

Jenny leaned into the fence, clutching the wires until they dug into her hands. The truth was she didn't even know and she wouldn't know —not until she stepped up to the plate, her bat sitting loose in her hands.

She just didn't know which of those two very different girls she'd turn out to be.

She had no idea what she wanted.

She closed her eyes. Yes, she knew. She knew precisely what she wanted.

She wanted a family, a home. Wanted to choose her own future, her own life. And more than anything, she wanted to open her eyes and see Jason sitting in the stands, watching her as he always did.

Smiling, like he always did.

She took a deep calming breath. But that couldn't happen. She had no control over that, but this… right now, this she had control over.

Jenny didn't know if Jason would be there, if he'd show up, and part of her was glad. She didn't know if she could do this, if she could stand to see his disappointment if she didn't live up to his expectations.

But wasn't that part of the problem? Her living up to everyone else's expectations and not her own?

Feet shuffled up to her, a small click, click in the dirt and Jenny knew exactly whose shoes those were. Shoes only one person would wear on a softball field.

Speaking of expectations….

Samantha Dawson.

"And here she is, the player of the hour. Do you have any words for your fans, Jennifer?"

Samantha stood there, wearing a similar, just-as-revealing, cleavage-induced, suit as the last one Jenny had seen. A predatory grin pulled at her lips, and with what that splattering of blood lipstick it really looked like she'd gone to town on some poor, helpless rabbit.

With Samantha, Jenny wouldn't have been surprised. Not in the least.

Samantha shoved a microphone into Jenny's face. "Well, Jennifer? Do you plan on making the softball hall of fame or do you plan on striking out as has been rumored?"

Jenny shifted back. The strain and tension drained from her face. She'd learned one thing from Alice and that was how to keep her cool in front of a nosy, giant cleavage reporter. And if Alice could keep her temper then so could Jenny.

"Ms. Dawson. I thought we talked about this last time?"

"I'm sorry, we actually didn't get around to talking much what with your fellow teammate —"

"Informing you of my age, which I assure you, is still under eighteen; and considering neither of my parents are standing next to me, I guess that means I don't have any comments."

"We can always get one."

"You do that. Me? I've got a game to play. I hope you enjoy."

"Well, that'll really depend on you won't it. But home run or strike out, I'll still get my story and where will you be?"

"Happy."

Jenny spun on her cleats and stomped to the center of the dugout.

All she could hope for was happiness. One way or another. She'd find her happiness. She'd find her own smile.

For whatever reason, the team crowded around her—separating her from Samantha and the rest of the fans. They didn't say anything to Jenny, and other than her brief chat with Lacey, they'd kept their silence. Even Alice, who now sat on the furthest end of the bench, tossing a ball into her glove, didn't bait Jenny.

Their support shocked her in a way Samantha and her camera couldn't. Made Jenny hesitate, unsure if whether or not she could see this through.

She didn't deserve this. Didn't deserve *them.*

Each one of these girls stood beside her, determined, faces set. Just days ago those faces had turned on her, had told her not to come back. And now… and now she was one of them.

Jenny shoved her hands under her arms pits to keep them from shaking. She couldn't think about them, not now. She'd lose her nerve if she did.

This was her one chance to show her dad, to prove to him just how badly she needed him to listen, to let her live her own life.

There was no other way.

Surprisingly, Samantha and her cameraman retreated to the stands without much of a fuss, but then Jenny realized exactly where Samantha was going—to get an exclusive from her dad.

He sat on the bench with her mom, both of their bottoms cushioned by special chairs her mom had packed for today. Seeing them there, sitting together, hands lightly clasped, hurt.

It was the first time her father had come to her game in years and the only reason he was here was to make sure she didn't screw it up.

Samantha waved as she came near, and after a moment, her dad's dark, several-hundred-dollar sunglasses turned on Jenny. She could easily guess what Samantha was saying, but she didn't care.

What happened next was her choice.

Jenny started the game as second baseman, just as Lacey had said, but before Jenny raced onto the field to join her team, she lingered, unable to take that final step.

Should she do this? Could she?

Alice tapped her on the back. She still wore her high-ass ponytail, and it swung behind her like a pendulum, but she met Jenny's gaze and for once there was no disdain, no scowl.

"It's not right what he's doing to you. Lacey didn't think you'd believe what she said, so I wanted to tell you." Alice took a deep breath, then let it out in one giant puff. Words rushed out so fast it took Jenny a moment to translate. "We'll back you up. Whatever you want, whatever you decide, we've got your back."

Jenny nearly fell over. She didn't, however, and instead found herself smiling back. The first real smile she'd given to Alice.

"Thank you. Knowing you're there...." her smile grew, made her heart warm. "It means I can do this."

That she could stand up to her father.

"Good. I still don't like you." Alice turned to right field, jogged a few steps, then glanced over her shoulder. "But we're a team; you do what you need to."

Jenny could. She would.

In the stands her father was deeply engaged with Samantha and her wiles, her pushed-up cleavage and low-cut shirt. Beside him, her mom sat straight as a board, hands clasped in her lap, face pale as she tried to ignore the flirting going on right beside her.

Jenny knew what she had to do. If her father wouldn't listen, if he wouldn't take a moment to hear her, to actually care what she had to say... then it looked like this was the only choice she had.

And yet, as she took the field with the rest of her team, her steps were light. The team was behind her. For whatever reason, they weren't letting her go through this alone.

She had no idea, not until she fielded the first ball Elizabeth tossed her and threw it back, did Jenny realize just how much she needed that —needed them.

She wasn't alone and she never would be again.

Lacey ended up pitching a hell of the first couple of innings and Mount Crest only got a few dinky hits off her. On the other hand, Mount Crest was pulling out their top guns as well. The score was still tied 0-0.

Tensions heated. The cheers grew louder, escalated until the stands joined in. Regardless of what she felt, of her own personal agenda, Jenny felt herself swept up with the team, pulled right along with them. Cheering, clapping, hoping in her heart that Mandy would beat-out the throw to first—and she did!

Jenny jumped up from the bench. Clapping, yelling. Only one out and she was coming up to bat.

Jenny threw on her helmet, grabbed her bat and gave it a couple of good, slow swings. She watched the pitcher, timed the right moment when the heel of her bat would streak out, then extend.

She felt the excitement, felt the exhilaration right until she heard her father's voice cheering her on. Clapping.

The excitement snuffed out and Jenny remembered why she was here.

Remembered what she needed to do.

Her softball spark, the one she felt moments ago, vanished. She got up to bat… and struck out.

A swing and a miss.

The crowd quieted, hesitated as if it didn't dare a breath.

Jenny kept her head down as she jogged back to the dugout. Didn't look at Mandy, now stranded on first and hoping for Elizabeth to move her to second base.

Jenny had seen the pitch, had seen the ball curve to the outside. She'd known what to do… and she'd swung too early. She'd known she'd miss.

The girls clapped her on the shoulder, just like they always did, but no one gave her any encouraging words, no one told her she'd get it next time. They knew she wouldn't. They knew she didn't want to.

And still, Coach Steele let her keep playing.

From the third base coach's box, Coach Steele merely nodded and it made Jenny's heart swell, made her want to cry. How was it these girls, this team she'd nearly torn apart, stood behind her while her father couldn't? While he sat with the reporter and glared at Jenny?

She ducked her head and wiped a tear before it could fall, before another could join it. Alice was beside her, not touching her but there none the less.

It made Jenny want to cry even more.

Even Alice, who hated her, understood. Was standing up for her.

"You'll get this, Jen. Just hang in there. Besides, you wouldn't want to disappoint your fired coach or your boyfriend would you? Not to mention my brother who decided to stop acting like a retarded ass. Thanks, by the way, for telling him he's a dick."

Alice grinned. Jenny didn't even notice. She jumped to her feet and her heart surged right along with her. Sure enough, there was Chuck, hands tucked in his pockets, leaning against the field's light pole. Behind him was the baseball team, who came out together as a group to support the girls, just as they'd done for them against Mount Crest. And wheeling along beside them was Dan. No, he wasn't smiling, but he wore his old uniform and his storm cloud seemed a little smaller than she'd last seen it.

But Jenny didn't have eyes for the team or for Dan. She couldn't look away from the player standing front and center. The player who strode towards her like he was meant to be there, like he was meant to wear that uniform, that hat… and those very tight, very attractive white pants.

Jason.

THIRTY-EIGHT

J ason."

He'd come. He'd come even after everything that had happened, after everything she'd said. Hope surged in her, locked in her throat. He had eyes only for her. Determined, caring eyes.

Lacey had said he loved her.

Breathing suddenly got very, very difficult.

"Heads up," Alice whispered as she slid behind Jenny. "Dad."

Jenny jerked attention away from Jason. Sure enough, her dad was storming towards her. He swept off his sunglasses in one motion and headed right for Jenny. Samantha was kicking her heels up behind him, trying to catch up.

This, Jenny knew, had to end.

If Dan could make that damn raincloud of his shrink, if Jason could throw aside his guilt and wear his uniform again, than she could stand up to her dad.

"I'm going out there."

"Not alone you're not." Alice blocked her way. Then one by one, the girls stood up. "But since we all can't go, Lacey and I will be your back up."

"You can't. I mean —"

"Shut it, Transfer." Lacey slapped a hand on Jenny's head. "Let's go tell your dad off. We got a game to win, remember?"

"Yeah, I remember."

And she did. A game she intended to win. But for herself. Not for her dad.

Jenny and her two shadows left the dugout, skirted around the edge until they met her dad on the other side of the fence. It felt right to have them there. The two girls who'd had the most to lose by Jenny joining the team—and the most to gain if she left. But they were there, by her side. It felt right.

The baseball team was in sight, but Jenny kept her eyes forward. She couldn't look at Jason. Not now. She needed all her nerves, all her steel, to deal with this.

"What the hell was that?" Her dad growled, not even bothering to keep his voice down.

"It's called a strike out, Dad. You know. You average those two or three times a game."

"Don't you take that tone with me, Jennifer. Do you have any idea what you looked like out there? How you're embarrassing me?"

Samantha whipped out her recorder. "How, exactly, Sam? Your fans want to know."

"His fans don't give a shit." Jenny snapped the recorder away from her dad and shoved Samantha out of the way. He towered over, like he always did, but not this time. This time she was going to tower over *him*. "His fans don't give a shit. It's his sponsors that do. The sponsors he's already set up to 'sign' my future away with."

"Oh?" Samantha crooned. "Like who?"

"Who," her dad growled, "doesn't matter if she keeps striking out at every time she's up to bat. This," he spat at Chuck, "this is all your God damn fault. If you hadn't —"

Jason, who she hadn't seen come over, slid between Jenny and her father. His arm snaked around her waist and held her to him. Even with all her rage, all her need to scream at her dad, Jason's touch sizzled through her, sparked through her.

Like Lacey and Alice, it felt *right* that he was here.

She couldn't help the smile, couldn't help her joy at seeing him. That he'd come, that he'd forgiven her. That he'd dared to stand up to a man as powerful and wealthy as Sam Taylor.

And seeing Jason was just the distraction her dad needed to forget Chuck and tear a new one into Jason.

"You! You're the one —"

"Who's in love with your daughter." Jason shot a hand out. "I'm Jason Richards. Good to meet you, sir."

At the word 'love' her dad's mouth dropped. Jenny's stomach also dropped and now she really felt faint. Behind them the dugout cheered as someone hit a hard ball into the field. Jenny had no idea who. Had no idea what kind of ball was hit or which base Mandy ended up at.

She didn't care.

Jason loved her.

"You…? Really?"

"Really." Jason dropped his hand and turned to her. The same smile she remembered, the smile Jason wore on that first Sunday at the ballpark. "From the first moment you stood up to my sister."

"Jennifer isn't allowed to have any boyfriends," her dad interjected. "Not while she's playing softball."

At *that* Jenny's head shot up. "Oh really? Well, I guess we'll just solve all the problems right here and now. I'm tired of your damn baseball career, Dad. I'm tired of you coming home at 4:00 in the morning with three shades of lipstick on your collar. And more than anything, I'm tired of you trying to control my life. I am NOT your legacy. I am NOT the Taylor baseball legacy."

"Jenny —"

"No. You listen to me. For once, *you* listen because I'm only going to say this once. After today, I'm done. Do you hear me? I quit. No more softball. No more future pro sports. I'm finished!"

"You will do no such thing, young lady."

But her mom was there, putting another calming hand on her dad's shoulder. "Let it go, Sam. She's made up her mind."

"Like hell she has!"

Except Jenny had. And she wasn't finished. "This team, this school, and this boy make me happy. They are my home, Dad. I'm tired of moving, I'm tired of starting over because you've decided to be an ass and get yourself traded to another team again. But I'm done. I finally know what a home is, and I refuse to give it up. Not for you. Not for your career. Not even for mine."

Never again.

Her dad's face fell. Shock slowly worked its way through him as if he finally, *finally* heard what she said.

The anger drained away and left behind the man who could be her father. Jenny didn't know, didn't know because she didn't know that man anymore. He'd been gone for so long.

"I… you really feel that way."

"I do."

He breathed in, let it out. Shock was still there, but she saw understanding work its way in. Slowly. "I didn't know. I wanted, I wanted what was best for you. I'm sorry."

"Yeah," she whispered, "me too. But I'm not backing down. I'm staying. Right here."

Beside her dad, Samantha continued to ask questions but he had finally tuned her out. She was still getting one hell of a story, but no one but Samantha seemed to care anymore.

"You, you really feel that way about me? About the game?"

"Every word."

Her dad seemed to shrink on himself and suddenly he wasn't so tall, wasn't so grand. Sure he stood there in his expensive, polished shoes, his designer shirt… but now they were just clothes. They no longer represented the man underneath them.

Her mom sobbed and put a hand over her mouth. She must have seen the change too.

Jason still held onto Jenny, and she was grateful for the support; didn't know if she could stand on her own feet or if she was going to start crying like her mom.

"You know," her dad said after a minute, "baseball isn't the only Taylor legacy I've passed on to you."

"No?"

"Yeah. We're stubborn too."

Yes. She could definitely see that.

"This is what you want? This? All of this?" He motioned to the field, to Lacey and Alice behind her, to Jason.

"Yeah. It is."

"Okay, then. Okay." He nodded once, then a second time. "Okay. A family. A home. I can make that happen. I've got to make a call to my manager and see what we can do to keep me here. See if I can extend my contract."

Relief swept through Jenny. She closed her eyes, barely trusted herself to say the two simple words: thank you.

But she said them anyway because she suddenly knew, for the first time in years, this was one promise he was going to keep. No matter what.

And now… now Jenny had her own promise to keep.

Two actually. One was to finish this game and be the softball star she knew she was… and the second was going to prom with Jason.

Two promises she had no doubt she could handle.

THIRTY-NINE

J enny fidgeted in front of the full-length mirror, a new purchase her mother insisted on buying for this occasion. She pulled at the sparkling blue, sleeveless fabric of her dress and wondered for the sixth time if she could get away with wearing jeans.

"You're fidgeting again."

Her mother tucked another of Jenny's curls under her chin. Curls she'd insisted on doing for prom—no, the *dance*.

"You look beautiful."

"I feel like an idiot." She'd felt less of an idiot after staring down her dad at the Mount Crest game, a nice loud 'discussion' that pretty much everyone had heard (or had a transcript of at this point). But they'd won. Jenny had gone on to fulfill her promise, to Jason, to the team.

They'd won.

But she still felt like an idiot wearing this… this thing called a dress.

"Well, in that case," her mother gave her another kiss on the forehead, "you look like a beautiful idiot who's going to knock that boy over when he gets a look at you."

Jenny smirked. "His name's Jason."

Still, Jenny couldn't help but take in the long, ankle-length dress that clenched around her thin waist and then swayed out from under her hips, dragging on the floor behind her. She turned around and gave her butt a good, hard look.

Not bad.

Alice had been right when she said the dress didn't make her butt look fat.

Good to know she had friends. Well. At least friends like Alice.

Jenny smiled.

Okay, maybe she didn't feel exactly like an idiot but she wasn't about to admit that to her mom—not after she'd taken her to the fifteen different dress shops and made Jenny try on two hundred dresses.

She wasn't even going to talk about Alice's screwed up delight about that. She should never have agreed to bring her along in the first place.

"You're frowning again." Her mom touched her nose. "No frowning. Not tonight."

"Who said anything about tonight? And who said I was even going to the prom, anyway?"

"That hair, make-up, and dress perhaps." Her mom quirked up an eyebrow. "You gonna go show your dad how beautiful you look?"

"I was hoping to sneak out the back."

From the doorway she heard her dad's hard steps pause outside her door. "Fat chance. You think I'm going to let a guy take my daughter out when she looks as beautiful as you? At least, not without a few threats?"

He smiled at her, a real smile. It was something she'd seen on him more in these past few weeks than in the past few years. Ever since the big game, since Jenny had stood up to him, since they'd talked. It had also helped that Jenny ended up smacking a curve ball into right field, going with the pitch just like Chuck had taught instead of trying to pull it. Her dad had surged to his feet, just like everyone else, and had cheered her on for the pure excitement—just like everyone else.

Even Samantha Dawson (who did get her story, but who no one but Dad's sponsors cared about) cheered.

Jenny didn't give a shit about Samantha Dawson. Not when her hit had been the game winning run. Not when her dad had turned and kissed her mom with the same pure joy, the same excitement.

Even now, he leaned in and kissed her mom on the forehead. Soft and gentle. Loving.

Jenny went back to fiddling with the dress that wouldn't seem to stay safely planted above her boobs. What was with this thing that it kept wanting to fall down?

She hiked the dress back up again.

This was *never* going to work.

"Stop fidgeting." This time it was her dad who said it.

"I'm not fidgeting. I'm just trying not to blush while my parents make-out in front of me."

But she smiled as she said it and they smiled right back as they made their way downstairs.

Her dad wasn't going to be alone in his worries tonight as Jenny went to prom with Jason (who her dad insisted was still too old for her, but her mother put her foot down on). Chuck was there too, feet kicked up on the couch, and gave Jenny an appreciative glance.

"I think this is the first time I've seen you dressed up."

"First and last time," she mumbled.

But Chuck grinned, just like he always did. He and her dad were watching the girls' professional softball game on TV. Not for Jenny and her future, but because they both agreed professional softball was important. It was a sport that should be invested in, should be an option for girls who truly loved softball, who wanted to play women's professional ball. Her dad wasn't going to give up on that investment, even if Jenny didn't want to play.

It made her smile—a smile that froze in horror when her mom opened the front door. "You ready?"

No. Yes.

"Can I throw up first?"

"Not in that dress you can't. Come on, Jenny. Your date's waiting."

Jason.

Dear God, what was she thinking? Could she really do this?

"I don't get it. How can I be okay with a crowd full of strangers staring at me on the pitching mound, and now I feel like running to the bathroom and losing my lunch."

Her mom whispered another kiss on her forehead. "Because. He's a boy. They have that effect on us."

Her mom kept up a cheery hum during the drive and Jenny tried not to peel off her newly painted nails. Yes, that was a little strange for Jason not to pick *her* up, but she needed to maintain some amount of control right? Still, just to make her opinion known, Jenny complained the whole way. Her mom hummed.

Somehow, it worked.

But it wasn't until she got to Jason's door that her smile crept back onto her face.

She was happy.

For the first time in years, she was happy.

Her dad had tried to give her the perfect future, a perfect life, a future filled with just as many opportunities as he'd had, but now Jenny was the one finally building her life.

A life, she hoped, that would include Jason.

The thought was nearly enough to freeze her, to make her pick up her skirts and run back to her mom's car.

She closed her eyes, breathed in, slow and deep.

All she had to do was step up to the plate, to hold her bat, light and easy in her hands, and swing away. If she never tried, if she never swung her bat and dared miss a pitch or two, then she'd never have a shot of hitting a home run.

In softball, or in life.

Jenny reached out and rang the doorbell.

The door opened instantly. Jason stood there, hands splayed on his hips, black tuxedo fitting him just as snug as his baseball pants and just as mouthwatering.

Holy shit.

It was a good thing prom only came around once a lifetime, otherwise she'd really be in trouble.

But it was Jason's smile, and not the suit, that made her head spin.

That—and his kiss, as his hands circled around her waist and pulled her to him. And still, even now, his touch, his kiss, sent wave after wave of sparks through her.

And she never wanted it to stop. The kiss. Or the sparks.

It was only when they came up for air did her head stop spinning. Sort of.

"About damn time. You're as hard-headed as my sister. You were starting to make me sweat if you'd show up or not."

Lacey shoved past the two of them. Actually her frilly—was that a pink dress?—shoved them out of the way. This, of course, only pushed Jenny further into Jason's very sculpted, very perfect chest.

"I told you, dumbass," Lacey snapped, "girls take a long time to get ready. Now hurry the hell up. I'm not about to wait here all night in these pinchy shoes while you two kiss. I happen to have a date, too, you know."

Jenny laughed. It felt good—no, right—to laugh. "I wouldn't dream of making you uncomfortable, Lacey."

Lacey snorted and headed towards the limo, somehow managing not to tip over in heels she clearly had no idea how to walk in. Especially when she walked on the grass and… got stuck.

The limo pulled into the driveway. Doors opened. Elizabeth and her date came out. Waved. Smiled. So did Heather and Mandy.

Her teammates.

Hers.

Jenny intertwined her fingers with Jason's. He turned to her, his grin just as handsome and breathtaking as ever.

"You ready to go to this stupid dance?"

Without a doubt, Jenny knew this time when she stepped up to the plate the ball was going clear out of the park. Going far out there, and never landing.

"With you? Absolutely."

HOME RUN

A HOME RUN NOVEL

Learn more about Laurie's past in *Home Run: A Home Run Novel*, on sale now from your favorite retailer. Turn the page for a sample chapter from that book.

In the world of girls softball, fun no longer matters. Colleges. Scholarships. Laurie Stevens fought this her whole life. A former college star who walked away from it all. Now, a coach for twelve-year-old girls, she faces the same challenge.

A challenge that hits home when former Major League Baseball player, Jack Evans, and his lonely daughter, walks onto her team and into her life.

"Home Run," a novel about dreams, romance, and, hope for the future.

"Wonderful book, chockfull of unexpected surprises. If you like sports novels, you'll like this—even if you don't like romance. If you like romance, you'll like this—even if you don't like sports novels."

—Kristine Kathryn Rusch, *USA Today* Bestselling Author.

ONE

The softball cracked off the bat.

Laurie slid to the edge of her overturned bucket. Nearly tipped herself over as she leaned, closer and closer to the chain-link fence. Her metal cleats scraped on the dugout's cement floor and she pushed as if she was the one turning and running, running to catch the high, flying ball.

Just like she'd done, hundreds, no *thousands* of times before.

Laurie gripped the chain-link separating her and the field she'd practically grown up on. Gripped it hard until her own memories, of pushing off the buzzed short grass and racing to make the catch, faded. Until it was just her and her team again.

Until it was just little Suzie Turner out in right field.

Suzie, with her bouncing pigtails and smile as wide as the field, turned and ran. Her deep pink uniform, with the white lettering of her last name and the number one, reflected the heating, sweltering sun. But despite the sun and its beating-down glare, Suzie hadn't been dozing or drifting off. Not this time. This time she'd gotten a good jump. Had seen the hit. Had seen the softball flinging in her direction; the very second it'd happened.

It would be close.

Very close.

Laurie watched as Suzie glanced over her shoulder. Took in the distance. And, like Laurie had taught her, kept on running.

"Come on. Come on," Laurie chanted.

The ball arched, high, then higher. On the field, the other team's runners sprinted for the next base. Flinging dust and dry dirt into the air until it formed a cloud so thick Laurie could barely track of that white speck in the sky.

It was either the winning hit. Or the losing hit.

Meanwhile her team, her wonderful amazing team, shouted. Called out to each other. Asked for who had it.

Suzie answered.

Behind Laurie, the roar and cheer of parents froze. A collective, indrawn breath like Laurie's. Like Hugh and the handful of girls beside her in the dugout. They all waited. Watched.

Suzie, still running, still pumping as hard as she could, stretched out her arm. Opened her worn, brown leather glove—and that flying, spinning softball landed smack in the middle.

Just like they'd worked on.

Just like they'd practiced.

Laurie leapt up from her bucket. Pumped a fist into the air and let loose a walloping cheer with Hugh and her girls.

And unlike anything they could practice, it was when Suzie turned, with a face filled with so much shock Laurie could see it clear from the dugout.

Along with that big, gigantic smile.

They'd won.

Won the game, yes, but for Laurie, and what really mattered, she'd won that smile.

Except Laurie heard the unmistakable *thump, thump* behind her. So loud, so clear, it dwarfed the cheering parents.

Laurie's own smile slipped.

She glanced over her shoulder, and sure enough, there was Dan Richards, jumping down from the bleachers—yes, from the lowest step—and waddling towards the dugout. His rolling belly, and the

Slugging Angels T-shirt barely tucked into his jeans, hanging on by the slightest fold. But it was the red, scrunched face, the glinting eyes that held her.

She swallowed a curse (always mindful of her words around her girls—regardless of the currently cheering, very loud bodies).

The dust from the softball's impact hadn't yet cleared, let alone the umpire's usual shout of, "Game over!" before Richards was ready to let her have it.

Again.

Along with spewing angry spit all over her.

Just great.

She knew exactly what this was about. And how it would turn out.

Laurie fingered the sunflower seeds in her khaki shorts pocket. Just looking at Richards gave her a sour taste. And his temper. She might as well add in a mouthful of salt... except, no. She needed to deal with this. And without a mouthful of sunflower of seeds.

Yeah, she'd deal with it.

And do it the only way she knew how.

The only way she could.

She smashed her pink, *Slugging Angels* ball-cap on her head, squashing her ponytail flat, and prepared for some good ol' coach-to-parent battle.

Hugh, her co-coach and team owner, leaned against the fence. His wrinkled, leathery face was already tanned from the unrelenting southern California sun, a tan that was always better than hers.

He noticed her attention. And who it was on.

"You got this one?" Hugh asked. "He's a bit high-strung today."

"Just today? Hell, I'm surprised he hasn't blown out his knees from all the bleacher-jumping he's been doing."

Hugh lifted his eyebrows, which disappeared into his white mop of hair. "Careful there, Coach. Never know who's listening."

Referring to the five girls streaming out of the dugout, screaming and cheering at the top of their lungs. Laurie smiled and shook her head. "I think I'm safe."

Safe from being overheard (for now), but not safe from a determined and angry dad like Richards. A dad who, at times like this, hit a little too close to home.

Laurie shoved aside the memories, but they latched on. Held her. Gripped her so hard that, for a moment, it wasn't Richards stomping towards her, sneakers brushing the reddish-brown dust into the air. Wasn't Richards wearing that complete, disapproving look.

A look that said no matter how hard she worked, no matter how hard she trained, it wasn't enough.

She'd never be good enough.

Except this *was* Richards.

Not her dad.

And he was yelling at her. A coach. His daughter's coach.

Laurie dug her cleats into the cement, scraping and squashing the memory away. She wasn't a player anymore. She was a coach; a *good* coach, and she just flat out didn't have time to deal with the past—not if she expected to handle Richards.

And be nice about it, too.

Dealing with irate, know-it-all parents required a delicate touch. It was an art, one Laurie had picked up over the years. She'd seen all kinds of softball parents, from the most understanding and loving to the kind who pushed their girls until the game of softball changed from a fun sport to a job.

Those were the kinds of parents Laurie wanted to slug. And with good reason.

It didn't matter how many of these parents she'd met over the years or how many 'talks' she'd had with them. It never got easier. The memories were always there, lurking, waking up at just the right—and the wrong—moments.

"Enough, Stevens," Laurie growled to herself. "Focus."

She'd have to use her best tactic. Quick and to the point.

And it was the only way she'd get through this with her shredded self intact.

Laurie grabbed her old, reliable, 25-ounce Louisville Slugger bat and went to head Richards off.

A good bat, one she'd used in her high school days and all the way through college. Still of use to her, even now, even after that career had long ended.

Her girls ran from the field and into the dugout, all nine mingling with the other five racing out. Leaving Laurie trapped in the middle.

"We did it, Laurie!" Suzie leaped in the air, hugging Laurie around the middle. "Did you see my catch?"

"I sure did. You were great!" Laurie leaned her bat against the fence, temporarily relinquishing its comfort, and held up both hands for the team's high-five jumps.

Parents were one part of her job, this was the other. The better one.

Suzie jumped, stretching her short fingers towards Laurie's hand, and completely missed the double high-five.

Not that Suzie cared, or any of the other girls for that matter. One by one, they jumped, missed, and then tried again. Hugh gave his usual deep, barrel laugh, the one their girls loved, before shooing them into the dugout to clean and pack up.

Richards reached the field, face red, steam practically spewing from his ears. That last fold from his T-shirt finally untucked and now flapped around his middle.

Time for business.

Laurie finished the last couple of air high-fives and hefted her bat.

Lacey, the only girl who hadn't lined up for the high-fives, was standing off to the side, cleats still on, glove still clutched in her fist. Refused to enter the dugout. She towered over the other girls, both in height and size. Already pitchers on the other team were sending Lacey wary glances whenever she stepped up to the plate because any bat of Lacey's that touched the ball practically ensured it would go far.

To the *fence* far.

And she hadn't even hit her growth spurt, which meant there was a good chance she'd be a hell of a hitter once that kicked in. Not much of a runner, though, and if that attitude kept up, she'd not be much of a softball player, either.

But it was the attitude that was the problem.

A big problem.

One that, if Laurie didn't get a handle on—and on *Richards*—

meant Lacey would go down a path darker than the one she'd gone down.

At least Laurie's teammates (when she'd played) had always liked her. At least they'd never been *afraid* of her.

Lacey gave Laurie a smug smile, the one kids got when they knew their parents were gonna knock some serious sense into you.

Hugh noticed Laurie's gaze and leaned closer, keeping his voice low and jolly so the girls wouldn't suspect trouble. "You sure? You know he wants Lacey to start more."

Laurie lifted her eyebrows. "You mean, this would go easier if you talked with him and not me?"

Which was true. Mostly because Hugh was male and to Richards's mindset, that meant he was much more willing to understand his position as Lacey's father.

But she understood his position just fine.

After all, she'd had a father just like him.

This was her team as much as Hugh's and whether she liked it or not, parents came with the territory. Even the ones that brought up bad memories.

"Thanks, but I'll handle this."

She needed to. Because, maybe, one day, she could move on.

Hugh glanced pointedly at the bat resting on her shoulder. "That's part of what I'm worried about, girl. You play nice, remember?"

"I always play nice." *When they do.*

Thankfully, she was saved from Hugh's response as the girls, Suzie in particular, had quite a few highlights of the game they were sure Hugh had missed seeing, and therefore had to enlighten him.

Lacey still glared at Laurie, still refusing to come into the dugout. Clearly she wanted to be near the action of her dad ripping Laurie a new one.

"Go get packed up." Laurie pointed into the dugout.

Lacey merely lifted her chin. Triumph.

Not today, kid.

With girls like Lacey, girls who thought they knew everything, there was really only one way to deal with them.

Be bigger. Stronger. Then maybe, somewhere down the line, they'd be willing to listen to something softer.

Kinder.

"Get packed or sit the next two games."

"That's not fair! I'm one of the best players. You need me out there if you want to win."

Laurie straightened. Took a deep breath to calm herself. Lacey was getting to be too much like Richards. The same arrogance. The same driving desire she'd seen countless times back on her old teams.

No matter how much she wanted to, she couldn't yell at Lacey. Couldn't even tell her how dangerous this road was and where it would lead if she wasn't careful. Because Lacey wouldn't listen.

Not yet. Maybe not ever.

For some girls, they never did.

"We're not here to win. We're here to have fun."

Lacey knew that. All her girls, and their parents, knew that. This was a team that had fun. The day it became a job for them was the day Laurie quit.

"Pack up or sit out. Your choice." Laurie spun, her cleats digging nicely into the hard-packed dirt, and headed Richards off before he reached the dugout.

This wasn't a conversation she wanted her girls to overhear.

But to appease Hugh, she gave Richards her best smile, though she did swing her bat nicely onto her shoulder. Might as well appeal to his male sensibility and appear strong. It might work in her favor.

"What can I do for you, Mr. Richards?"

"Coach," Richards growled. "This is the second game you've sat my daughter."

"Actually, I was pretty sure she was playing first base just now."

"You know what I meant." Sweat streamed from his face and his giant nostrils flared. "She should be starting. No one else on this team can pitch or hit like Lacey, and you sat her!"

Laurie's smile wobbled as her temper flared. "You know very well why I sat her."

"Do you think I'm just going to sit around and let you ruin my kid's chances? Ruin her shot at a great future?"

"Dan. Your daughter's twelve. She isn't even close to the age where—"

"Every game is important! Every game she has a chance to catch someone's eye. A coach on an 18-and-Under Team even."

"Eighteen? Christ, Richards, she's only twelve!"

But he didn't hear her. Couldn't. Already too lost in big dreams and an even bigger future.

"Maybe even scouts. High school. Hell, college. *And* if you can't teach her, if you can't be the great coach we thought you were, then you're wasting our time."

Her head swam.

Richards was honest to God thinking of Lacey for an 18-and-Under Team?

When it came to travel softball teams, age didn't exactly matter. Travel teams were the intense version of this game. More than any school or high school or league team. These were the teams that traveled to different cities, different states even, all with the end goal in mind: playing for college.

Just not Laurie's team.

Which was why she was coaching girls so young. Young enough that those big, lofty dreams didn't matter. Having fun was what mattered.

But if you were good enough to play with the big girls, and on those teams where seniors dominated, then you'd play with the big girls.

If you were good enough.

If your parents agreed it was the right move.

Laurie couldn't think of one instance where it was the right move. Not for a girl barely twelve. Not for Lacey.

It certainly hadn't been for Laurie.

The field tilted slightly. Red-brown dirt and the green, trimmed outfield temporarily trading places. How many times, for how many of her own years playing softball, had she heard Richards's exact words? Those exact same dreams?

Sometimes, they'd even come from her own, misguided lips.

Richards stepped forward, breaking the hold her past had on her. She needed to focus. Needed to be right here, right now if she was going to do Lacey any good.

She had to talk him down.

Laurie didn't back up. Not even when he pressed close enough she could practically taste his own sweat on her tongue. She squeezed the comforting rubber on the bat's handle. Dirt slid under her nails.

Focus. Stay calm.

"You still think you're some great hot shot?" Richards continued. "Well, I got news for you. You ain't in this sport anymore. You're a has-been, and the fact that anyone even remembers you playin' is a miracle."

This time, he leaned so close their noses nearly touched.

It took all of Laurie's control not to slug him. This man, no matter what she said, no matter what she did, would never understand.

Would never listen.

And *that* hit too close to home.

Enough to re-stir her anger. To push through the air that was trying to hard to catch in her throat. To clog there and keep her captive.

Not this time.

Not ever again.

"So you tell me," Richards growled, so close the sweat from his brow heated the already sun-hot air between them, "who the hell do you think you are sitting my daughter?"

"Her coach."

Laurie tapped her bat gently on her shoulder.

A reminder.

Richards's eyes zeroed in on it, but he made no move to back down or back up. Not like she'd expected him to.

"I'm the coach," she said again. "Lacey's coach, just like every other girl on this team. I'm also not going to stand here and let you yell in front of these girls. You have a problem with the way I run this team? You don't like the way I coach? That I don't measure up to your inflated expectations of me? Fine."

Another tap of the bat.

Richards's eyes jerked back to her face. They widened. Just slightly. As if *finally* realizing the danger.

That, just maybe, he'd gone too far.

"When Lacey joined this team, I made myself clear. We're not here to train your daughter for college ball. My girls are here to enjoy the game, to have fun." Laurie's breath hissed out, low and dangerous. "And if you ever yell like that in front of my girls, you and Lacey can get the hell off my team."

They glared at each other.

Richards looked away first.

Laurie risked a glance at the dugout. Hugh had done his part, keeping the young-ins away, focused on the small candy bars he was handing out on account of their second win of the season.

Even Lacey had been distracted by the promised treats. Good. Meant that they could finish this before it got any worse. Of course, quite a few of the parents had crept closer, hoping to overhear.

That was at least one thing that never changed from team to team, or parent to parent.

The gossip.

Laurie leaned back. "Do you have any problems with that?"

It was a trap question, and the way Richards's eyes narrowed, he knew it too. He and Lacey could quit the team; that was their choice.

She didn't resent them for it, but this was also her team.

She had choices too.

"Now," she gestured towards center field. "Why don't we have that talk, take a short walk, and work this out?"

She brushed past him. Her hand tightening on the bat. *Patience. Just another parent, one who if all the signs pointed correctly, wouldn't last long.*

Parents like Richards never did. They always had their own ideas, their own big dreams for their kids. The kind of dreams that usually ended up with two words: *college* and *scholarship*.

Why was she even doing this? Why was she fighting so hard when no one wanted to listen? What was the point?

They reached center field and Laurie thrust aside all her doubts. Richards would sense them, like a shark smelling blood.

Their talk went about as well as expected. Richards was furious Laurie hadn't started Lacey (again), and of course, was adamant that when Lacey had shoved their catcher Mandy, it was not in fact, a shove.

"Shove or not a shove," Laurie said. "I don't give a shit."

Richards's mouth clicked shut. He blinked. A softball coach for twelve-year-olds didn't do much swearing. It came with the job. There were times, however, when such words were needed.

Necessary, even.

Like now.

"A gentle, friendly shove is still a shove and I won't have fighting on my team. I warned Lacey and she decided to back talk to me. So, I benched her for the first half of the game. Hugh agrees with my decision."

That last comment effectively cut Richards off at the knees. He couldn't go plead his case to Hugh, not if Hugh was already on Laurie's side.

"If you want her playing," Laurie said, "then I suggest you talk to her."

Lacey's fighting habits had started almost immediately after her parents separated. That, however, wasn't Laurie's business. There were certain topics where it wasn't her place to say anything. At least not until kids like Lacey made it Laurie's business.

Richards might not be pleased, but he couldn't argue her points. He didn't say he agreed with her; no, that wouldn't be up his alley, but he nodded anyway and went to collect his daughter.

Lacey had that gleam in her eyes, the triumph for having her dad stand up for her, which immediately died when Richards shook his head.

Not this time, kid, Laurie thought to herself.

Of course, Lacey had no idea, and would never know, that the real person who'd stood up for her had been Laurie.

She watched them leave and the muscles in her right shoulder pulsed. She rubbed at the knots and hissed. A leftover reminder from her softball days, the muscles still hurt, still got tense whenever something like this happened. As if her body, along with her mind, refused to let her forget.

She lowered her arm. Right now, the last thing she needed to remember was playing softball and dealing with her dad, the coach.

"You gonna help me out here?" Hugh came up beside her and dumped a handful of softballs into the bucket.

"You bet." It was exactly the kind of distraction she needed. She and Hugh loaded up the ball buckets and equipment bags into the back of Laurie's somehow still running pick-up.

The weekend hadn't been a hard one, not for their team, anyway. Only two games on both days, though the spring season was only just getting started. They'd be soon seeing their girls once during the week for practice, then on the weekends. Switching between three and four games a day, every week until the summer season closed.

Still, the park—with its four, well-used softball fields—was already deserted. Teams, parents, and their kids seemed to vanish the second the last pitch was thrown. It made the park more relaxing, more inviting as if it needed the quiet to settle in for the night after a long day of roasting hot dogs, French fries, and mounds of ketchup.

But right now, with her shoulder pulsing and Richards's accusations rolling around her mind, not to mention her own damn memories, the last thing Laurie felt was peace.

She packed her bat and slammed the tailgate door. Her truck shook slightly.

Hugh lifted his eyebrows at her. "It went that well, huh? Got a bit of extra steam to work off?"

"Steam is too generous. Try really pissed off."

"I can see that. You want to talk about it?"

"No."

Hugh merely looked at her.

"There isn't much to say. I told him to back off. Lacey pushed Mandy, regardless of how he wants to dice it."

"I noticed he stopped yelling."

Laurie shrugged. "Not hard to do when you carry a bat."

And if you have no problem using it, if push comes to shove.

Hugh let the bat comment slide. But he looked at her, like he always did. Just like he always knew why she needed it for these talks.

The bat, as much as the softballs and the very fields her team played on, were part of her past. A direct link, and a reminder, of the kind of coach she refused to be.

"You okay?"

She knew what he was asking. And why.

"Yes. No." Laurie leaned against her truck and rubbed her shoulder, the muscles still tight, still pinching. "It'll come up again. It won't be the last talk."

"Unless he decides to take her to another team." Hugh sighed. "I'm getting too old for this. It didn't always used to be this way, you know? Parents thinkin' they know what's best, even if they don't know anything about the game."

"It's not you. And it's not me. The game's changing."

It had started to change when she was Lacey's age, when it was Laurie out there being yelled at by her father as he pushed her to do better, to excel.

She rubbed her forehead. What was wrong with her today? Why all these memories and why now? Was it just because of Richards?

Sure dealing with him usually brought on the bad times, ones that no matter how many times she buried them, just kept digging themselves free.

"I thought I could change things, make a difference in their lives."

Hugh reached over and gripped her shoulder. "You are. Why do you think parents keep lining up to join?"

They joined because regardless of what Richards thought, Laurie and Hugh were excellent coaches. They had a knack for bringing up the best talent, for nurturing girls. The problem was she and Hugh were merely the dinosaurs who refused to go extinct. That was the real problem. The one neither wanted to bring up.

Teams nowadays didn't care about having fun. They wanted results. They wanted the best chance for the kids to get that college scholarship.

It didn't matter if the kids were only twelve-freakin'-years old.

Laurie bit her tongue and kept her thoughts to herself. So did Hugh.

One day, they'd have to accept it, but until then well it didn't matter so much did it?

"Still," Hugh reached his arms up above his head, his old bones cracking and creaking as he stretched. "Sittin' all day on that damn bucket—I'm definitely too old for that."

"Whatever you say, old man."

Hugh laughed. "Old? Damn straight I'm old. Girl I remember when you were no taller than our Suzie-pie. About just as freckled too."

"I was always taller than Suzie. And I only had two freckles." She knew because she'd counted nearly every day.

Hugh scanned the empty parking lot, a lot that had been recently filled with the more expensive cars and BMW's. That was southern California living for you. Laurie's beat-up truck was the only one of its kind on game days.

"But you're right," he said. "Times are changing. It's not the same game as when you came through. A different world." He shook his head. "More kids will be like Lacey, more dads like Richards who think they know everything."

Laurie dusted off her pants a final time, not like it did much difference. She seemed to be covered in as much dirt as her girls. "It's still enough the same."

She hoped it was, that there was enough reason for her to stay, to keep playing the game she used to enjoy so much. "As long as there are kids who want to play good ball, who want to have fun, then I'll still be here."

She'd still coach. She'd make sure at least one girl had the experience she never did. As long as she never crossed that line, the line that so many coaches had no problems stepping over, she'd keep coaching.

Yes, she still spent most of her days helping out kids—or trying to. Most kids, especially the lovely high school age ones Laurie taught, didn't appreciate the help. But out here, on the field, this was still her life.

Even as hard as that life had been at times.

But she'd learned, the hard way, that she couldn't stay away.

This, *this*, was where her heart was.

On the field.

"I know you will, kid." Hugh slapped her shoulder. "I've no doubts about that."

Laurie nodded, but kept her mouth shut. She had her doubts, and Richards in all his anger, had reminded her of them.

To continue reading "Home Run," visit ChrissyWissler.com or your favorite bookseller.

Any Normal person thinks magic a myth. Anyone worth knowing, knows differently. Magic wanted and it took. Free pizza delivery, free Wi-Fi, freewill.

All of it, fair game.

Blessa of the Blessings Bridge made sure all her landing platforms, from the golden arches to the inter-dimensional voids, remained clear of seaweed and seagull shit. An important job, really. Essential, even.

Too bad she hated it.

"The Blessings Bridge" will transport you to living, breathing world where magic resides alongside freeways, fishing piers, and funnel cakes. A world you never knew about, but always knew existed... right outside your backdoor.

To enjoy your free copy of, "The Blessings Bridge," go to: chrissywissler.com/free-book/

Keep up with the latest news, releases, and much more at chrissywissler.com.

ABOUT THE AUTHOR

Chrissy Wissler's writing has garnered praise both from readers and professional writers. Readers love her characters and the emotional grip she engenders.

About her novel *Home Run*, *New York Times* bestselling author Kristine Kathryn Rusch said: "Wonderful book, chockfull of unexpected surprises. If you like sports novels, you'll like this—even if you don't like romance. If you like romance, you'll like this—even if you don't like sports novels."

Chrissy's short fiction has appeared in the anthologies: *Fiction River: Risk-Takers, Fiction River Presents: Legacies, Fiction River Presents: Readers' Choice, Deep Magic,* and *When Dreams Come True*. She writes fantasy and science fiction, as well as a softball, contemporary series for both romance and young adult.

Before turning to fiction, Chrissy also wrote nonfiction for publications such as *Montana Outdoors, Women in the Outdoors*, and *Jakes Magazine*. In 2009, *Inside Kung Fu* magazine awarded her with their 'Writer of the Year' award.

Follow her blog on being a parent-writer at Parents and Prose.

To enjoy another story by Chrissy Wissler and to keep up with the latest news, releases and more, go to: chrissywissler.com/free-book/

For more information:
www.chrissywissler.com
chrissy@chrissywissler.com

Hidden in Fire

Hidden in Flight

Hidden in Spirit

Hidden in Desire

Hidden in Memory

Hidden in Time: Novel

Hidden in Lore: Collection #1

Hidden in Myth: Collection #2

Hidden in Legend: Collection #3

Enchantment Avenue

Searching for Sanctuary: Novel

Dragons in Preschool: Short Novel

The Blessings Bridge

Pixie Dust Cupcakes

Christmas Weather Witch

Unfreeze a Heart

More than Nurture

Romance Video Game Series

Second Chance: Novel

Anything Possible

Changing Perspective